SHAYLA BLACK
Dangerous Boys
and their *Toy*

ELLORA'S CAVE
ROMANTICA PUBLISHING

What the critics are saying...

An Ellora's Cave Romantica Publication

www.ellorascave.com

Dangerous Boys and Their Toy

ISBN 9781419958502
ALL RIGHTS RESERVED.
Dangerous Boys and Their Toy Copyright © 2008 Shayla Black
Edited by Sue-Ellen Gower.
Photography and cover art by Les Byerley.

This book printed in the U.S.A.

Electronic book Publication May 2008
Trade paperback Publication February 2009

DANGEROUS BOYS AND THEIR TOY

છ૭

Trademarks Acknowledgement

ℰↃ

Chapter One

❧

"Now that we're out in the middle of nowhere, crouched outside a house I've never seen, you want to tell me why you dragged my ass here?" Detective Cameron Martinez glared over his right shoulder, through the inky mountain darkness, at bounty hunter R. A. Thorn.

"Julio Marco's trial starts next week. No one can find the star witness."

"Tell me something I don't know." Cam clenched his fists, hard-pressed to keep his voice to a furious whisper. "Without Curtis Lawton, the D.A. doesn't have much of a case, Julio Marco will go free, and my ass will be in a sling."

"Yeah? I'm Lawton's bail bondsman, and he's not checking in like he promised. If he fails to appear I'm out something close to fifty grand. That's not chump change."

True, but at least Thorn wouldn't have to explain to the victims smuggled from Mexico and sold into slavery why Julio Marco, the man responsible for their torment, wasn't going to prison for a very long time, as promised. Or why Curtis Lawton, the man who helped Marco, was nowhere to be found. That would fall on Cam's shoulders.

"It wasn't my idea to give the asshole the option of bailing out. Judge Nelson needs to have his head examined. And I advised you against posting Lawton's bond, if you recall."

Thorn shrugged. "I knew he was a flight risk. I had no doubt he'd do whatever necessary to avoid prison time and those unsavory pals of his who know he's turned snitch. But I've hunted him before. That's why we're here. I found him in this cozy little bungalow last year, boffing out his girlfriend's

9

brains."

"This her place?"

Thorn shook his head, the long ends of his golden hair brushing his wide, solid shoulders. "His. He moves girlfriends in to fuck them, and out once they're history. I did a drive-by earlier today. He's got a new hottie shacked up here. Pretty, young thing. Little, long brown hair, world-class ass. Lawton has crappy taste in occupations but good taste in women."

Who cared what she looked like? "Can you please keep your dick out of a conversation for once?"

Thorn's icy eyes mocked him through the darkness. "Sure, Saint Cam. As soon as the little woman makes her appearance, let's see if you can keep your dick out of the conversation. I'm telling you, she's fucking gorgeous."

Right now, Cam cared about the fact that come next Monday, if Curtis Lawton didn't live up to his plea deal and testify against Julio Marco, his former boss, two years of Cam's work would be down the toilet. And a lot of young Mexican Nationals who endured utter hell on earth after being guaranteed a golden ticket to the promised land would be left without justice. It figured that Thorn couldn't get his mind off sex for more than ten minutes strung together. Why should anything be different today?

"Whatever." Cam felt free to roll his eyes in the dark. "What's the plan?"

"We wait. As smokin' as this woman is, good ol' Curtis won't stay away long. I sure as hell wouldn't."

That went without saying. Thorn constantly thought with his penis. But he also never thought about the same woman more than a handful of times. Good thing for him he was a good-looking SOB who could melt a woman's panties on looks alone. Thorn was long on bad-boy temper and short on sensitivity and charm.

"I don't care if she's Miss America," Cam returned. "She's being kept by a scumbag and making her living on her back by servicing a criminal. The idea of taking Lawton's sloppy seconds doesn't get me hot."

"You're too picky. It's a miracle you ever get laid."

"It's a miracle *you* get laid," Cam countered. "It's so impersonal for you, it's like a drive-through window, man. `Would you like just the screwing, or do you want the combo package? That comes with a nipple squeeze and a tongue fuck.'"

"No one's had the need to ask me to supersize in order to get off." Thorn bristled. "I haven't heard complaints."

"You don't stay around long enough to know if there are any. I know you're never going to tell me your full name, but do you make every woman you nail call you by your last name? Or is it like all your legal documents, Mr. R. A. Thorn?"

"Fuck you. They don't need to know my full name to get off. And I'm not there for a *relationship*. It's just sex." He scowled. "Are we here to catch Lawton or hash out my personal life?"

Cam shook his head. As much as it pained him to admit it, Thorn was right. The man's fast-food sex life was none of his business. It certainly wasn't what he would have chosen, and he had suspicions that the big blond hulk was achingly lonely, but would never admit it. And Cam couldn't make him.

"Let's catch Lawton. Do we know anything about his girlfriend?"

"Other than her fine ass or the fact she has the kind of tits that make a grown man beg, no."

Figured Thorn didn't get a name. Half the time he didn't bother when he took a woman to bed. Why learn the name of one he hadn't even touched?

Before Cam could answer, the ground lights flipped on at the back of the bungalow, casting a muted golden glow over the trail to the pool. Then a willowy woman emerged, wearing a thin white robe belted around her small waist. She held a towel in one hand, a glass of wine in the other. Shutting the door behind her, she sashayed down the trail to the pool, closer to their hiding spot in the dusty bushes.

After setting her towel on the chaise and her wine on a nearby table, the woman checked to make sure her hair was still secured on top of her head by some clip Cam couldn't see. Satisfied, she gazed up at the vast black desert sky and its many blinking stars, the majestic view unfettered by the city's lights. She smiled faintly—then dropped her robe. She was completely naked.

Cam sucked in a breath.

"Holy shit," Thorn muttered beside him, his voice suddenly sounding as if he'd been eating gravel. "I was hard just wondering what she had on under that thing. But now…"

He had been, too, Cam admitted silently. But seeing the real thing, her endless ivory skin, pert handfuls of breasts with wide nipples, the graceful curve of her hips… Holy shit seemed like an understatement. Despite the fact she was willingly sleeping with one of the worst dregs of society, Cam still felt a pull to her he could barely process. For once, he and Thorn agreed on something.

"Shh," he said instead.

No need to admit that he wanted her too. If she was the kind of woman who'd let a creep like Lawton pay her bills in exchange for sex, she was the kind of woman who would fall for Thorn's casual sex line. In other words, easy. Cam knew he'd still be trying to learn her name and something about her by the time Thorn was zipping up his pants and saying goodbye.

Thankfully, Thorn didn't make more conversation. His gaze appeared permanently glued to the woman's nipples, hard from a light teasing by the cool evening breeze, which was finally tolerable now that October was only days away.

Without hesitation, she swayed toward the pool and stepped into the water with a long, low sigh.

The ache in Cam's groin tightened at the sound. Did she make little sounds like that when she was aroused?

Beside him, Thorn growled.

"Shh," he reminded with a glare.

Thorn totally ignored him.

The beauty submerged until only her head remained above the surface. She kicked from one end of the pool to the other, moving with a slow grace, unhurried, as if she had all the time in the world to devote to this pleasure — or any other.

Unfortunately, Cam was all too aware that he didn't have all the time in the world. The trial started in mere days.

"As enjoyable as this is," he whispered to Thorn, "how is watching Miss America here get naked going to help us find Lawton?"

"Like I said, you don't think he'll stay away long from her, do you?"

No. Good point. In fact, he was no more than twenty feet away from her and pissed off that bushes and dark water obscured his view of her amazing body. He could only imagine how a man who'd touched every contour and sampled every inch would miss those graceful, supple curves.

With a long sigh, she swam to the edge of the pool and ascended the stairs, hips and sweet ass swinging as she made her way up, until she was completely exposed to the night air.

With quick efficiency, she patted herself down with the towel. Cam had never been so envious of terrycloth. Then she tossed back the rest of her wine in one quick swallow and lay on the chaise, face raised to the silvery moon.

Gorgeous. Like a goddess. All toned limbs and soft skin, with a graceful curve to her neck, an intriguing tilt of her head. She looked untouched. Untouchable.

Until she planted her feet on either side of the chaise, parting the firm length of her thighs, and smoothed a palm down her soft abdomen — and right between her legs.

13

"Fuck," Thorn snarled under his breath.

Cam clenched his jaw. Again, he had to agree, especially when she made lazy circles with her fingers over her mound.

Under her touch, her hips moved slowly, restlessly. Her head fell back, exposing the column of her white throat. Her pouty mouth parted and her breath caught on a gasp.

She moaned.

"Fuck."

"Shh," Cam reminded Thorn again, though he noticed his own tone was definitely more than raspy. Funny how a raging hard-on could change a man's voice.

Thorn clenched his jaw, looking ready to charge through the bushes, rip off his pants, and fuck her blind. That wasn't Cam's usual style, but the idea now held major appeal.

Especially when she moaned again and plunged her fingers into her pussy. Wishing he could see her better was quickly becoming an obsession. He wanted her so bad he hurt. How wet was she? Did she shave or wax? Was she swollen? Did her fingers fill her hungry sex? How tightly would her pussy grip his cock?

"Bet the carpet matches the drapes," Thorn whispered.

Cam didn't usually care about such things—it was the person inside who mattered to him—but in this case, something about the woman made all the rules different. And he suspected Thorn was right. There didn't seem to be anything artificial about her, from the unaffected sensual sway of her hips to the natural weight of her firm breasts, now rising and falling more rapidly.

A sharp, sudden catch of her breath split the tense night air. Cam swallowed a groan and feared his cock would bust out of his jeans when she spread her knees wider and again raised her hips to her invading fingers.

"Fuck!" Thorn whispered harshly, adjusting his erection in his pants.

The bounty hunter's frustration might be funny, if Cameron wasn't in the same situation. Damn, a few minutes of watching her touch herself and already his balls felt tight, like he could shoot off at any moment. He wasn't some damn randy teenager, but watching her made him feel like one.

Her breaths got shorter, harsher. She worked herself furiously—until Cam was breathing hard, felt himself sweating, despite the sixty-degree evening.

"That's it, baby," Thorn coached in a whisper. "Fuck yourself. Deeper. Oh, yeah. God, she looks sexy. I'm so damn hard, I could pound nails."

"Just don't ask her if she needs any help."

The woman raised one hand to a hard nipple stabbing its way into the cool desert air and pinched it. She gave another long, low moan that had Cam biting his lip.

"Wouldn't dream of interrupting," Thorn murmured. "Hell of a floor show. Let her get nice and wet and pliant, then I'll offer to soothe her with my tongue."

"TMI," he muttered.

But the conversation ended when she shoved her fingers even harder into her pussy, grabbed her nipple in a hard pinch, then gyrated, moaning in a series of whimpers.

She looked poised on the edge, ready to explode at any moment. Cam held his breath, grasping the edge of sanity as he watched her fast movements grow frantic, almost panicked.

She let loose a frustrated wail. Even at this distance, he could see her trembling thighs, her body so taut that every muscle vibrated with need.

But she didn't come.

"Can't she get off?" Thorn asked.

The beauty answered that question with a jerk back of her head, a pounding of her fists on rigid thighs, and a discouraged cry that echoed through the little courtyard.

Moments later, the cry became a sob as she gathered her

knees to her chest and lowered her face until all he could see was the thick coil of her caramel-colored hair and her shoulders shaking with the force of her tears.

Her aroused mewling had reached out and gripped his cock with need and impatience. This...her sobs, they clawed at his gut, tore at his heart.

A hand on his shoulder startled him. He turned to Thorn in question.

"Sit back down, Dr. Phil, or she'll see you. You can't go barging over there to dry her tears. You'll blow our cover to hell."

Cam nodded, taking a deep breath. He'd been so far gone with the desire to hold her and help her, he'd nearly given their presence away? Not good. At all. But he couldn't deny that some part of him ached to kiss the lushness of her mouth that darkness only hinted at, replace her fingers with his, then watch her come apart in his arms. He'd keep her tight against him if the need for tears came again.

The urge was utterly stupid.

Exhaling raggedly, Cam clenched shaking hands into fists. She was a criminal's mistress. Whatever her issue was, it was none of his.

"Sorry," he murmured.

Thorn was already on another subject. "Think she needs pain to get off? I know from seeing Lawton's last honey that he sure can dish it out."

Grimacing, Cam tried to avoid a mental image of this beauty begging toilet scum like Lawton to hurt her. But he couldn't discount the possibility that Thorn was right. What other explanation was there for her inability to orgasm?

"I don't know but it's not why we're here. Let's focus."

"Hard to focus when all the blood in my body has gone south of my belt buckle." Thorn grimaced.

Cam rolled his eyes. "Manage—quick. We need a plan. I

hate to tip my hand too early by dropping in to question her."

"But we're running out of time."

"Yeah." Cam couldn't ignore that reality.

Lawton's girlfriend sniffled and lifted her face to the desert night. Silvery tears marred the smooth apples of her cheeks. He couldn't see her eyes in the dark but the sadness that bounced off her, the despair that ate at her—he could feel it, thick and dark. Dejection pulled at her shoulders as she rose slowly, taking the towel in one hand, empty glass of wine in the other.

Even a view of her heart-stopping ass couldn't cut through Cam's urgent need to hold her, help her. Something was completely wrong, and he was dying to know what.

But she disappeared into the house without giving him a single clue.

At his side, Thorn released a long, hard breath. Cam wondered how long he'd been holding it.

"That girl needs to get off. Bad. I volunteer help, even if it takes all night." Thorn's sly grin grated on his nerves.

"Shut up, you moron. She doesn't just need to come. Whatever is bothering her is deeper than an orgasm will solve."

"Not my problem."

"Fuck them and forget them, huh? Nice motto." Sarcasm grated his voice.

Thorn gritted his teeth. "I can't stand you pussies who are in touch with your emotions."

"I can't stand you assholes who can't think past your cock."

Silence descended, a full five minutes of it. In that time, crickets chirped, frogs croaked, while the desert wind kicked dust up into the bushes providing their cover. Lawton's girlfriend turned out the lights at the back of the bungalow.

And Cam felt guilty. He and Thorn had been

acquaintances for a long time. Not great friends. Thorn never let anyone very close. But still, sort of friends. Squabbling over the man's sex life was stupid. Neither one of them would likely ever have sex with Lawton's girlfriend—much less get to help her with her orgasm deficit, more's the pity.

Before he could open his mouth, Thorn said. "Fuck this, dude. Let's get back to the case. I want to keep my fifty thou and you need your witness for court." He hesitated, looked away. "You're one of the few friends I've got. I don't want some chick getting in the way of that."

Cam turned to Thorn, and he knew shock was all over his face. "That's the nicest thing you've ever said to me."

His stare turned glacial. "Don't try to interpret my emotions, pussy."

That was like asking Cam not to breathe. He probably knew them better than Thorn himself did. Then again, Cam had four sisters. If he hadn't learned to think emotionally, he would never have survived to adulthood.

"Whatever, asshole," he said. "I think we wait twenty-fours, then see if Lawton shows up. If not, I'll pull out my badge and pay his pretty little mistress a visit."

* * * * *

Brenna Sheridan saw nothing but red.

Rearing back, she eyed the big punching bag dangling from the ceiling, the tight grip of the boxing gloves around her wrists a familiar bite. She swung, putting every bit of her fury and frustration into the punch. Her fist connected with a satisfying thud, and the red bag dipped and swung. The impact of the blow shot fire up her arm. With clenched teeth, she grunted, but Brenna refused to feel pain. She'd been at this for an hour, and she wasn't done.

Leaning back on her right leg, she kicked her left out to the bag, connecting with a vicious jolt that sent a punishing thud echoing through the room and a thrill of satisfaction zinging through her.

Sweat poured down her temples, between her breasts, down her back, dampening her white tank and black spandex shorts. Tendrils of hair floated near her face, having escaped the haphazard clip she'd shoved them into. With a toss of her head, they disappeared, leaving her free to step forward and punch out with another hard jab at the offending bag.

She pretended instead it was Curtis Lawton's head.

Rude, insensitive, downright stupid... Then again, he'd been that way for years. She shouldn't be at all surprised. He'd come around—but in his time, his way. He always did.

Brenna danced around the bag, balancing on the balls of her feet, before she lashed out with a fierce right kick. Because of him, she didn't trust men, didn't know how to really be herself when she was with them. She'd let him get in her head and mess with her mind. Stupid! And last night... Damn, by the pool with the stars twinkling, a glass of wine relaxing her body, she'd still been unable to come! And the source of her problems? Gone. Would a phone call hurt the man? He'd kept her at arm's length in Texas forever. He'd occasionally sent birthday gifts and actually called last Christmas. Nothing else. So she'd come to him here in Arizona. She'd been here all of fifteen minutes, and what did he do? Disappear.

Bastard.

This morning, the reason for his behavior had become crystal clear. She'd read the morning paper, and dear Curtis' name was plastered all over the front pages with lurid headlines: *Local man to turn evidence in slavery ring.*

Brenna had read on in shock. What the hell had he gotten himself into? According to the article, he'd helped smuggle young Mexican men and women into the U.S., then forcing them to work for a pittance in everything from sweatshops to underground bordellos. The whole thing turned her stomach.

After ensconcing her in this pretty little house in the middle of nowhere, he'd vanished, so it wasn't like she could ask him any questions. He'd merely given her some warnings that made no sense—go nowhere, trust no one, say nothing. Then he'd gone.

Breathing hard, Brenna jerked her arm back and thrust it forward again, landing another solid strike directly on the heavy red bag. Her shoulder ached and her body trembled from the exertion but it felt good. Even if it didn't do much to calm her mind.

What in the hell was she going to do about Curtis?

A loud, impatient pounding on the little bungalow's front door snapped Brenna's head around. She hesitated, her breathing harsh. If Curtis had returned, he would have just barged in.

That meant a stranger knew she was here. Out in the remote mountains of this austere desert, it wasn't as if she had any neighbors welcoming her to the area with a plate of cookies. Whoever hammered on the door with a rough fist definitely wasn't female or here for a friendly chat.

Too bad for them she was in a foul mood and had no intent to let anyone screw with her.

Drawing off her boxing gloves as more impatient raps on the door resounded through the place, Brenna darted down the hall and searched the French Provincial nightstand in the sumptuous bedroom until she found what she was looking for. Ah, a Beretta. Lovely semiautomatic favored by military and law enforcement. Curtis did love his guns.

This ought to deter her uninvited guest.

With a smile and the gun clutched tightly in her fist, Brenna sauntered to the front door.

Chapter Two

∞

Brenna yanked the door open, the Beretta firmly gripped in one hand. Bad attitude, as only a Texas girl raised with macho alpha male cousins can conjure, was stamped all over her face. She wasn't sure what she expected. Leather-wearing goons with jagged scars on their faces, maybe? Nothing, though, could have prepared her for the man who stood under the dim porch light, badge in hand.

Tall. So striking she couldn't breathe for fully thirty seconds. Wow! Six-two...six-three. He towered way, way above her. Hair a silky, unrelieved black that looked as if it had been cut short once, months ago, then left to hang loose to brush his collar and tangle across his wide forehead. Bronzed skin covered the landscape of an angular face, complete with a sharp jaw, a sensually sculpted mouth, and killer cheekbones bequeathed to him by some Apache ancestor. Eyes a swirl of mysterious colors, like whiskey with chocolate made smoky by a hint of sin lurking just under his calm façade.

Dear Lord, had she ever seen a more gorgeous man?

Shoulders nearly as wide as the doorframe stretched a tight gray t-shirt to the brim with muscles that bulged and rippled, despite the fact he did nothing more than breathe. Without conscious thought, her gaze strayed lower, over ridged abdominal muscles that even clothing couldn't conceal. And lower...to an impressive bulge nestled in clinging jeans that had faded in the most intriguing places. Forcing her gaze down again, she took in scuffed black western boots.

This guy gave the motto "Ride 'em, cowboy" a whole new meaning.

He cleared his throat. "Ma'am, I'm Detective Cameron

Martinez of the Tucson Police Department."

Detective, not just a beat cop. With what Curtis was into, it was a miracle they hadn't sent Border Patrol, INS, FBI, and a slew of other government agencies. But no, just the one absolutely amazing, beyond drool-worthy hunk.

"Would you mind putting the gun down?" he asked, his voice soft and forceful at once.

Oh, Lord! She'd been so busy gawking at the man, she'd forgotten she was pointing a weapon at him.

With an awkward smile, Brenna reached around and placed the Beretta on the small table against the wall on her left—but still within reach. "Out here all alone, a girl can't be too careful. How can I help you, Detective?"

Brenna tried to play it cool. Tried like crazy. Hard to seem calm with a trembling voice, damn it. He was going to ask her questions. And she wasn't a good liar. If she screwed this up, what the hell would happen to Curtis? Of course, if he did half of what he was accused of doing, he deserved to do hard time, but she needed his help before someone sent him behind bars. After last night, she knew she needed help real bad.

Besides, Curtis had told her not to trust *anybody*, even the police. For all she knew, Detective Martinez was a dirty cop.

Her unexpected visitor simply sent her a questioning glance, then changed the subject. "Can I come in and ask you a few questions?"

"Am I in trouble?"

She was stalling. Damn it, a story, some story—a believable one to throw him off track. She needed one now. No one would believe what Curtis told her to say...

"Not at all," he soothed.

"Um, as you can see, I'm in no shape for visitors." She looked down at her own sweaty garments and grimaced. "Maybe later?"

Great first impression. Pointing a gun at the man while

looking—and smelling—her worst. Now she had to choose between putting him off or lying about a criminal. She doubted there'd be any first dates in their future.

"It won't take long, ma'am. Or I don't mind waiting if you want to clean up first."

And let him look around Curtis' little hideaway while she showered? Not a good idea.

"Well, if it won't take long, now is fine." She stepped back to admit him.

Now what? Brenna blew out a deep breath, her mind racing. Calm. Yes, she had to stay calm. Or Mr. Tall, Dark and Unsettling would pick her apart in twenty words or less.

She led him to the small living room at the front of the house and perched on the edge of a chair. He chose the sofa across the room and stared at her with those unusual swirling eyes, giving away nothing of his thoughts.

Intense. Quiet. Perfect descriptions of him. "Gotta watch out for the quiet ones," Aunt Jeanne had always said. Looking at the detective, Brenna suddenly understood why and couldn't have agreed more.

"Can I get you something to drink?" She stalled again.

"No, ma'am."

"Brenna, please. When you say ma'am, I start looking for my aunt."

A corner of his mouth tipped up. And what a mouth! She'd been so mesmerized by his eyes earlier, she'd barely acknowledged the wide mouth that looked oh-so capable of sin.

"Brenna."

His deep, smooth voice gave her shivers. How would his whisper sound in her ear as he was thrusting deep inside her?

No. He was here to ask questions, not seduce her. She should be coming up with a believable story, not fantasizing.

"Last name?" he asked.

"Sheridan."

"You live here?"

"I'd planned to visit, stay awhile. But I'm from Texas originally."

That smile on his lips crept up a little farther. His eyes warmed. "I gathered that from your sweet southern accent."

Brenna tried not to blush under the weight of his gaze. Impossible. His stare centered on her, not exactly sexual...but not purely professional either. Especially when his gaze dipped for just a moment from her face to her breasts. Shit! She was wearing a thin white tank top, damp with sweat, and no bra. Knowing those enigmatic eyes of his were trained on her breasts hardened her nipples. Brenna didn't have to look down to know that they stabbed the front of her shirt, impossible to miss, and that he was getting an eyeful. From the subtle appreciation in his gaze, he liked what he saw. But to confirm, she lowered her lashes—and looked at the front of his jeans. Holy cow! Up straight, beyond hard. And his size...he'd crossed the line from impressive to imposing.

So the good detective realized she was female. That gave her an idea.

"Southern accent?" She batted her lashes at him. "I don't hear it. Everyone I know sounds like me."

He laughed, discreetly drawing his gaze back to her face. But his stare remained heavy, as if she was a puzzle he needed to solve. As if he knew just enough about her to intrigue him.

"Who are you visiting?"

"Curious?" she asked in soft challenge, shooting him a flirtatious gaze. "Why is that?"

"Not because I'm flirting, Brenna." His expression turned neutral. "It's my job."

Yes, his job. Of course. Well, she'd apparently failed in the subtle department. Being too obvious in her attempt to distract him from questioning her—not good. She held in a sigh. Well, lacking a better idea, there was always Curtis' story...

"I'm visiting Curtis Lawton. This is his place. But you knew that, Detective."

He acknowledged that truth with a nod. "What is your relationship with him?"

"I'm his mistress but I think you knew that too."

The detective paused, pondering his next words. "Lawton is much older than you."

"And much wealthier."

His jaw clenched. His biceps hardened and bulged with tension. But his eyes betrayed nothing. "How did you meet?"

"Mutual acquaintance. How is this relevant?"

"Do you know where he is?"

"At the moment? No."

"Do you have a way to reach him?"

"No. He…drops in when the mood strikes him."

"You don't even have a cell phone number? An email address?"

"I'm not his secretary. And I'm not in love with him. I'm merely a convenience for him. He comes by when he wants to take advantage of that fact."

He paused, mouth pressed into a thin line. For some reason, her answer pissed him off. Interesting…

"You're a beautiful woman who could do better."

Wow, talk about a change in tactics. Now what? She could usually think of a flippant answer, but not when his stare heated up and fastened on her. Not when his scorching gaze caressed her mouth, drifted down her jaw then returned for a long, unabashed stare at the hard tips of her breasts poking her tank top. His stare only made them harder. Brenna sucked in a breath.

"I'm interested in someone…good."

Sure, he would take that to mean Curtis, but she'd love to explore that possibility with the good detective. He looked very, very good, with all that amazing appeal and equipment. Maybe with him she could climax. She could just imagine him without a stitch of clothes walking toward her, all hard body and stiff cock, tall and demanding in that silent way of his.

Oh, just the thought was making her wet.

He crossed his arms over his massive chest. His gaze turned laser-sharp, unwavering. Nerves danced in her belly, arousal danced lower.

"I see," he answered in a slow drawl. "I just never thought of his predilection as good, and you don't look like you'd be into that."

Oh, hell. What else was Curtis into that she didn't know about? "Don't judge a book by its cover."

"Fair enough." He shrugged. "On a purely personal note, since you're into his scene, what does he do that turns you on? I'm curious. Can you describe it?"

His face remained blank, but something about the way he delivered the question challenged Brenna. *Shit!* He was toying with her, playing a game of cat and mouse. Now he was springing the trap. Clearly, he knew something about Curtis' life that she didn't. This cover story Curtis had suggested was a stupid one, and she'd known that from the get-go.

Brenna stood and sent him a frosty glare. "That question is a little too personal, Detective."

He unfolded his well-muscled body from the sofa and stood, then crossed her room until he stood right in front of her. "C'mon, we're adults. Tell me what you like about the things he does to your body."

Not a clue. She didn't even want to think about what Curtis did. "E—everything."

"Hmm. That right?"

The detective sent her a long, measured glance. He didn't say a word, but Brenna feared he didn't believe her.

Close. He was too close. So close she couldn't think of

anything to say that would convince him, not without knowing Curtis' "scene". So close, she could smell the musky, summer-rain scent of his body. Clean and but complicated—a lot like she suspected the man himself was.

She swallowed, caught in his dark stare. "Yes, that's exactly right."

He moved so fast, Brenna never had a moment to fight back. One minute she stood facing Detective Martinez, the next...she could feel him all along her back. He'd grabbed her arm, whirled her around, snaked a heavily veined forearm about her waist, and dragged her against his hard-muscled body, his erection pressed firmly against her ass.

Then he cupped her breast in his hand, just like that. Boom, he was touching her intimately. And she liked it. Loved it.

Brenna gasped. God, his hands were hot and enormous, covering her whole breast. His harsh exhalations on her neck sent shivers down her spine.

Cat and mouse, she reminded herself. *This is some sort of game to him.*

"What the hell are you doing?" she snapped.

He didn't answer with words. Instead, he took her stiff nipple between his thumb and finger—and gave it a cruel squeeze.

"Ouch!"

She wriggled for freedom—with no luck. His hold was unyielding, absolute.

"Get your hands off me!" she shouted.

"You didn't like that?" His silky question taunted her as he relaxed his grip on her nipple.

"No. Let me go, damn it!"

"Ah, I understand," he breathed into her ear, strumming the pebbled tip with his thumb.

Back and forth, over and over, until tingles leapt and

sizzled within her breast. Her knees nearly buckled. Her stomach jumped with a bolt of thrill. He most certainly did understand if just the soft pad of his thumb against her nipple made her wet.

Against her better judgment, a moan escaped her.

"I'll bet you need it harder."

Before she could protest, he squeezed her nipple with even more force than before. She yelped, her body going rigid. She blindly lashed out with her feet, trying to connect with his shins, instep—anything to make him let go.

"No! It hurts. Stop!"

Instantly, he released her and stepped away.

"Not your cup of tea?" he drawled.

"You bastard! I didn't ask you to—to grope me. That's got to be against rules or regulations or something. I'm going to call, find out who your boss is, and have your balls on a platter."

That little smile tilted the corners of his mouth again. "I'm sure they'll be happy to talk to you. Of course, they'll ask you about Curtis too. And they may not be as patient as I am. They might just take you right down to the station and see if you'd rather talk from behind bars. Aiding and abetting *is* a crime." He shrugged. "It's up to you."

He didn't even wait for her reply. Instead, the infuriating, gorgeous man stepped around her, leaving her gaping.

At the door, he turned around. "Oh, and when you talk to Curtis, tell him he'd better show up to the courthouse on Monday."

Then he left, and she stood there and in stunned silence, torn between ogling the scrumptious view of his backside and worrying that he'd call a whole passel of cops...who'd be a hell of a lot less kind if they suspected she'd lied.

* * * * *

When Cam dropped by the trailer, Thorn could see he was agitated. And sported a hard-on he couldn't miss.

This ought to be interesting.

He smiled at the thought and perched the corner of his ass on the rickety metal table in his six-by-six kitchen. "So what happened?"

Ducking to enter the little trailer, Cam slammed the door behind him and crossed the room, shooting him a glare of pure venom. He reached for the fridge, took out a longneck, and tossed half of it down his throat. "Damn it!"

"I followed you and tried to watch through my binoculars, but once you went inside, *nada*. So spill it. What went down? Any good news?"

"She's lying about virtually everything."

"Shit. I was hoping for some good news. She looked freshly fucked when she opened the door."

Cam glared, and Thorn kept his grin to himself. Yanking the chain on the man's temper was just too easy. "She'd been exercising. Did you notice that she greeted me with a gun in her hand?"

"Hmm. Missed that. Too busy looking at her tits."

Gritting his teeth, Cam shook his head, then he drained the rest of the bottle. "She told me her name and the fact she's from Texas. She admitted that she knows Lawton. Those are the only things I believe. After that, the truth got murky. She claims she's Lawton's mistress."

Thorn crossed his arms over his chest. If there was one thing he'd learned to appreciate about Cam over the last few years, it was the man's instinct. He'd risen through the ranks fast to become detective because he paid attention, could think with cool logic, and because he just seemed to understand people and see under their surfaces in a way Thorn envied and couldn't possibly duplicate.

"What makes you think it's bullshit? Lawton does like them young and hot. She qualifies."

29

"She was nervous, not only like she was hiding something. Nervous like she was confused. She tried to dodge me with flirtation. When it didn't work, she tried a bit of the ice princess routine, but she fumbled with it."

"Like, she's not that type?"

"Yeah. But the kicker... You're sure Lawton is into giving pain and wants women who can take it?"

"With what I saw last year, no question. He made sure when he fucked the bitch that he was causing her loads of pain. Floggers, nipple clamps, the whole nine yards. And she was lapping it up."

"Then the woman I just talked to isn't his mistress. She is *not* into pain."

"How'd you figure that out?" He drilled, wishing like hell he'd been a fly on the wall, watching Cam press the pretty liar for the truth and lose his control... He got hard just thinking about it.

"You're not getting details, pervert. I'll just say that, at one point, she wanted my balls on a platter."

"Holy shit, you go alpha on her?" Now *that* was a sight he'd pay money to see. Cam alpha. Who'da thunk it?

Despite his teasing yesterday, Thorn knew his pal did real well with the ladies. The few he knew Cam had taken to bed all sighed and swooned and flushed when he entered a room. They were fucking starstruck. He damn near laughed watching them try to get Cam's attention. They used words like "gentle" and "patient" and "perceptive". But Thorn had long suspected Cam had a kick-ass alpha side that some woman would bring out someday—when she rattled his cage enough.

And Thorn did love to see Cam with his cage rattled.

Cam looked away with a guilty expression. "I pushed her a little."

"She made you hard as hell."

He closed his eyes and sighed. "I'm not proud of it. But I proved that she's not into pain. Does it automatically mean, though, that she's not his mistress? I mean, she *is* living in his fortress of fornication."

Thorn laughed. "Yeah, but if she isn't into pain, then she isn't Lawton's little honey. I think Lawton needs to dish out pain to get off."

"Maybe. If we assume this woman isn't his mistress, it begs the question, why is she there and why would she lie?"

"Yeah, and if she doesn't need pain to get off, why couldn't she come last night?"

"Who the hell knows?" He sighed. "It's not relevant, anyway. We need to find out what her connection to Lawton is."

"Yeah, just not as much fun." Thorn winked. "Does she know where he is?"

Hesitating, Cam appeared to ponder the question, weigh things in his mind. "That one...maybe. She said no, but that was also when the ice princess act started. I think we go with the assumption that she's got *some* clue."

"Sounds reasonable." Thorn nodded. "And if she does, she'll tell him we're sniffing around."

"Lawton should know we're after him, anyway."

"True. Well, give her a few hours, go back there, and try her again. Maybe she'll cough up the truth."

"I can't."

"You have to."

"It won't work. She's hiding something, I'm sure of it. But she also knows I'm on to her. I had to do something...questionable to get the little bit of information she gave me. To get more, I'd probably have to do something that could get me arrested."

"Nah, man. You couldn't just question her? She could fuck up when you do, Cam. You can wear her down. I've seen

31

you do it with suspects. Just use all that cool patience."

"Around her, I don't have any." With a sigh, Cam rose, paced. "She's too...soft and curved. Hell, she fit right against me. That sweet Texas accent of hers went straight to my cock."

Thorn laughed. "Now you know how the rest of us guys live. Welcome to reality."

"This is serious!" Cam snarled. "If I'd spent another ten minutes alone with her, I would have found some way to get her clothes off, get her on her back, and fuck her senseless."

Grinning, Thorn decided then that's exactly what should happen...as long as he had a ringside seat. "Do you think she knows you're watching her every move?"

"Damn it, stop smiling. This is not good! Of course she knows I'm watching. She's not stupid."

Of course she wasn't. Even better. She'd give ol' Cam the runaround, make him hard and crazy. Make him see how every other red-blooded man lived his life. Maybe then, Cam would shut up about how much Thorn lived his life through his dick.

"And if you try to visit so you can question her again," Thorn said, "Even if you could keep your dick to yourself, she's simply not going to answer, right?"

"That pretty much sums it up. I need another beer. Then I need to get my head together and figure out what the hell to do."

Thorn couldn't miss the fact that, when Cam stood again and yanked the fridge door open, his erection stood as tall and thick as it had the minute he entered the trailer door.

"Well, if you tried your way of questioning her and didn't get all the information..." Thorn retrieved his Glock, his sunglasses, and the keys to his Harley from the rickety kitchen table. Then he flashed Cam a dangerous smile. "Maybe it's time for me to question her. My way."

Chapter Three

🔊

Brenna woke suddenly, to the feel of something around her ankle. Her cat? Winky rarely left her hiding places long enough to fraternize with the enemy. Was she cold?

Fighting sleep, Brenna managed to crack open her eyes. With a frown, she glanced around the dark, shadowed room. Where was she? Certainly not in her own bedroom.

Then it clicked—Arizona. The bedroom in Curtis' bungalow.

Which meant that Winky was back in Muenster, Texas with her aunt, not prowling around her ankles.

So what had she felt?

Opening her eyes completely, she gave the room a thorough scan. Black corners and unlit nooks surrounded her, but that didn't freak her out.

What did was the feeling that she wasn't alone.

The air seethed with a vibe she didn't understand—and couldn't ignore. Dark, intense, sexual. How weird... Had she been having a dream she couldn't shake? Maybe, but she didn't remember it.

Her palms began to sweat. Adrenaline eked into her system. She gave the room a harder stare—and still couldn't see a damn thing.

"Curtis?" she called hopefully.

"Guess again."

The unfamiliar male voice from across the room sent ice dashing into her veins. His tone wasn't much warmer either. Fear rooted her in place.

"Oh my God."

"I don't think He's going to help you tonight. Right now, it's just you and me."

"Who are you?" She heard her voice tremble.

He laughed in answer.

Brenna tried to get up, dart out of the bed. No go. Her ankles had been spread and secured to the bedposts. Something jerked at her wrists and rattled near her ears.

The intruder had tied her ankles down, secured her wrists with handcuffs. *Oh, shit.* Was she going to wind up on the five o'clock news in a segment about a horrific murder, featuring some recent picture of her and a body bag?

She struggled again, frantically tugging at one wrist then the other. But the bite and metallic jangle let her know she wasn't moving.

"Those are standard-issue police cuffs," said the stranger as he stepped from the shadows, into the pool of moonlight under the skylight. "You're not going anywhere until I release you."

She could see enough about the intruder to get a general impression. He was a dream and a nightmare at once. Black leather pants, a matching vest…and nothing underneath but smooth bronze skin and rippling muscles. Oh, and the tattoos. They covered his left arm and shoulder in some intricate black flame pattern that wrapped around his enormous biceps multiple times, almost to the elbow. Blond hair hung straight to his shoulders. A silver medallion dangled from his neck and glinted in the moonlight between solid pecs and brushed the top of taut abs.

In another setting, this very bad boy would have made her incredibly wet.

Uninvited in her bedroom with her all tied up?

She screamed.

Calmly, he crossed the room, then covered her mouth

with his hand. "You know no one can hear you since your nearest neighbor is half a mile away. If it makes you feel better, I'm not here to hurt or kill you. I'm a...friend of Curtis'."

Yeah, wild hunch here, but friends of friends didn't tie one another up.

Brenna closed her mouth against the unfamiliar salty tang of his skin and jerked her head away, but her mind raced. Hearing that he knew Curtis didn't fill her with a warm fuzzy.

"As you can see, he's not here."

"I need your help finding him."

"I-I don't know where he is."

"Now, see, that's where I think you're lying to me."

She looked back at him, her eyes pleading in the dark. "No, I swear. A detective came by today. I told him I didn't know too. And I don't. I arrived here Saturday morning and he left fifteen minutes later. I don't know where he went. Honest."

There was a long pause. The stranger didn't step back or take his hand away. After she'd turned her head, his palm had settled on her neck, long fingers wrapping easily around it. God, that made her nervous. He could cut off her windpipe with a good squeeze.

"Know when he'll be back?"

"No. How do you know him? What kind of trouble is he in?"

He glided his palm over her shoulder, his thumb brushing under her tank top, perilously close to her breast, before running a light finger slowly down her arm, leaving a trail of unwanted tingles behind. He reached the handcuff around her wrist, binding her to the bed, and gave a playful tug. "I don't think you're in any position to be asking the questions. Let's try again. How do you know Curtis?"

"I-I..." She didn't dare float the mistress story again. If the detective had seen through her quickly, despite the dark, she couldn't possibly hope to hide anything from this predator.

"You...what?"

She stubbornly refused to answer. What could she say when she knew the lie was ineffective and the truth, at least according to Curtis, could land her in a heap of shit.

"It's a long story."

With a smile that did not comfort her, he crossed his arms over his wide chest. "I have all night. So do you."

As long as she was tied up this effectively? Yes. "I barely know him. Friend of a friend sort of thing," she improvised. "I came out here for a change of scenery. I certainly don't know anything that would help you."

Her intruder said nothing for a full minute. Instead, he reached down to inch her tank up her body to reveal her stomach beneath. He swept a broad palm over her skin, fingers snagging on her belly ring.

"You're a young, gorgeous girl. Long hair, tight ass, great tits," He punctuated the statement by lifting his hand over her bare breast and flicking her nipple, still hard and sore from the detective's cruel pinch. She gasped as pleasure jolted through her body.

Brenna heard fear and desire could affect the body in very similar ways. Tonight, she was getting firsthand proof. Why else would her nipples be hard if her life was in danger? Heaven help her if he discovered she was wet too. He'd tamper with her just for the joy of messing with her body and head.

Then, who knows? He might kill her for the sport of it.

Before she could protest, his hand settled high on her torso, just beneath her breast, which brushed the top of his hand. There, he planted, clearly with no intent to leave soon.

"Who are you?" she demanded.

He ignored her. "You know, you're just the sort of girl

36

Curtis likes to bring here to fuck. Is that why you're here?"

Curtis didn't live here? No wonder this cottage lacked all personal items or any sort of homey clutter. "No."

"I think I'll test, just to be sure you're telling the truth."

The intruder reached for her again. She had no idea what he intended to do, but if it was anything like what she'd endured earlier that day, she didn't want to find out. "No! Please...don't hurt me."

The biker paused. "So you know what Curtis is into?"

"Based on the conversation I had earlier today with the detective, I guessed. I-I don't know from experience."

An odd smile crossed his face. "The detective told you Curtis is a sadist?"

"No, he grabbed me and squeezed my..."

Brenna had a bad feeling if she explained the interaction between she and the hot detective that this intruder would want to test her reaction for himself. God, she didn't want to repeat that pain.

"He demonstrated," she corrected.

"Did he? He squeezed your...what?"

"That's not relevant. Aren't you here about Curtis?"

"We'll get back to him in a moment. The detective interests me too. He's usually a good little Boy Scout. Tell me how he inflicted pain on you."

She shook her head. "I'm not telling you so that you can do it for yourself."

"I don't like causing pain. I'm not a sick fuck, like Curtis."

"Really?" Sarcasm sprayed out like a garden hose full blast. "You only like to break into a woman's bedroom, tie her up in her sleep, then fondle and scare the hell out of her."

"Oh, I haven't even started to fondle you yet."

"Don't touch me!" The words sounded much braver than she felt.

He went on as if she hadn't even spoken. "I'm wondering..." The intruder eased his hand back to her breast, where he cupped it with a blazing palm. Then he set that thumb back over her nipple to graze and roll it back and forth. "Did he squeeze this one?"

Yes. And even now, she could feel the stranger's touch acutely through the remnants of the detective's pain. She was more sensitive than usual. Way more.

"Stop it!"

"It doesn't feel good?" he asked innocently as he thumbed the hard nub. "Did Detective Martinez squeeze this nipple?"

It felt too good. No way she was going to answer him, not when he'd take that as an invitation.

Suddenly, the bed dipped with his weight as he sat beside her. "I've been watching this place for a few days now. Give me some information about Curtis, and I'll give you the orgasm you couldn't give yourself by the pool."

Her jaw dropped as she drew back in horror. "You saw that?"

"Live and in living color. I know exactly what you're missing. Tell me what I want to know, and I'll give it to you."

"You can't," she blurted.

No one could. Something inside her just froze up every time she tried to come. By herself, she felt silly, the exercise pointless. With a man, she couldn't be in the moment. She simply focused on the inevitable "goodbye" before it even happened. The relaxing and enjoying they always suggested just never materialized.

For a few years in high school and college, she'd slept with any guy rumored to be well hung or good in bed. Nothing. This intruder, a potent mixture of danger and edgy sex appeal, who hadn't even told her his name, was even more temporary than most. He could be a cross between Valentino and a porn star and it wouldn't matter. No way could he get her to come when every other man had failed.

"Try me," he drawled.

His confidence made her shiver. Yes, a lot of guys had seemed as if they were proud of their bedroom prowess, and some had been better than others. This one... She wondered exactly what he had to back up his conviction.

Brenna shook off the thought. "Not to challenge you, but seriously, you can't make me come."

He just laughed. "If I do, you tell me about Curtis' whereabouts and your relationship with him. Deal?"

Talk about a bargain with the devil...

"And if you fail, you'll go away and leave me the hell alone?"

"Sure. Whatever. So, it's a deal?"

Rolling her eyes, Brenna sighed. "This is pointless. You can't make me come."

"I can."

Absolutely not. She was not going to invite a total stranger who had tied her to her own bed fondle her just in case he could finally give her the orgasm she'd been missing all her life. She wasn't.

"Prove it," she tossed back.

God, she hated when her impulsive tongue got the better of her common sense.

"If I do, you'll tell me what I want to know?"

Since what she knew was next to nothing, and he'd never make her come anyway, why not agree? Besides, every moment he was fondling her was a moment he wasn't trying to kill her. And a moment she could be looking for some way to escape.

"Yes."

"This is going to be fun."

She saw a flash of white teeth in the dark. No doubt, he

was awfully pleased with himself. As badly as her body would love the gratification, her head knew there was no way he'd be doing anything but eating crow. Then maybe, he'd unbind her. Hopefully. If not…she'd cross that bridge when she came to it.

The stranger reached down, disappearing from her line of sight for a moment. He returned, holding something she couldn't identify in the dark. He pressed a button, and after a *click*, a short, sharp blade gleamed in the inky air between them.

Her eyes widened, and she gasped. "I-I told you, I'm not into pain. Or blood. Or death."

"Me, either. But a guy's gotta do what a guy's gotta do…"

The intruder lowered the blade to her torso, beneath her tank top. Brenna's heart pumped frantically in her chest, and she could barely hear his words over the roar of blood in her head. She tried to thrash away but every limb was too secure. If she kept that up, she wasn't going anywhere—except to see Saint Peter.

He fitted the blade under the cotton and made his first cut—into the shirt, not her flesh.

"To see great tits," he finished with a laugh.

The asshole! He'd been toying with her, enjoying her distress, knowing all the while he had no intention of killing her.

Relief and anger poured through her at once, flooding her system with something dark and unfamiliar. He yanked up with his arm, his biceps bunching and bulging. The fabric of her shirt began to rip, a little more each time he sawed at it with his imposing strength. Finally, the blade sliced its way through the bottom of her shirt and the cool air teased her bare nipples.

"Holy shit." He dropped the knife beside her on the bed and stared at her in the muted moonlight. His gaze was almost reverent as he cupped the breast the detective had abused earlier that day. "Cam pinched this nipple, didn't he? Hard."

Brenna gave him a shaky nod.

"How hard?"

"I don't think I've ever felt anything that painful, especially the second time."

"He did it more than once?" Incredulity colored the intruder's voice, then he smiled.

Brenna was confused. *Cam*, he'd called the detective, as if he knew the guy. Did he? And why did he care about the way Cam had touched her?

"Were you even a little bit aroused?"

What an odd question. Was there a right or wrong answer? Did he want to know that Cam had turned her on? Under normal circumstances, she didn't think any man wanted to know that another had aroused her. But with this stranger, she got the distinct impression that knowing Cam had affected her would please him.

"When he just touched me, before he pinched...yes." In fact, in the moments before he'd delivered the pain, she'd thought his touch was one of the most pleasurable ever.

The intruder laughed. She'd didn't get the joke, but didn't think it was smart to ask him let her in on it.

"He touched you first? Tell me how."

"H-how? Ah...well, he put his hand on my breast."

"Just walked up to you and did this?" The stranger enveloped her sore breast in his palm.

"No. He grabbed my arm and spun me around, so his front covered my back. I...I could feel his hard breaths on my neck and every ripple of his chest when he exhaled. He reached around me and..."

"And you liked it."

That wasn't a question. Brenna didn't reply.

"You've been helpful already."

He bent down and placed a kiss on her abdomen, then his

tongue stole into her navel. Unexpected tingles darted down low, and her belly quivered. Her womb clenched.

"Hmm. Responsive," he whispered on her skin. "I like that in a woman. Let's see just how much."

Already he'd gotten more out of her than some guys had after a whole hour of sex, but that hardly meant he was going to be the man to incite her orgasm.

He kissed and nipped his way up her torso then laved her abused nipple. Blood filled it in a rush so quick, it was almost painful...but a sweet sort of pain. She gasped.

"Nice. Very responsive."

Before she could absolve him of that notion, he laved her other nipple. As if grateful to finally get some attention, it stood straight up almost the instant his tongue touched it. His thumb came behind him and provided enough delicious friction to make her catch her breath.

"Stop. This has gone far enough." Brenna tried to sound authoritative. Instead, she sounded like a quivering, half-aroused headcase.

"Unless you have very sensitive nipples, I can't make you come like this. We have a deal. You reneging?"

"I-I... You can't just..." She sighed in frustration. "It's not a real agreement."

"The hell it isn't. The chance to make you come in exchange for information. Or to get rid of me if I fail. Those were the terms."

"You can't mean to hold me to it."

"Why not? First, it's a great score to see you completely naked. I have every inch of you to myself. Second, it's the only way you're getting me out this door before I have what I want."

And tied down to the bed she wasn't in any position to refute him.

Getting rid of him wasn't what her body wanted, but

what would be best for Curtis and her own self-preservation? As much as she didn't want her gorgeous intruder to know that she was a freak who couldn't come like a "normal" girl, she wanted him gone more.

"Why do you want Curtis so badly, that you'd seduce an unknown woman in the middle of the night?"

"Believe me, honey, you're no hardship."

"You're not answering me."

"It's not something you need to worry about. We have unfinished business, Curtis and I."

"His business is dangerous. Do you know what he's been up to? Are you involved?"

"Yes and no, in that order."

"I certainly didn't know before I read it in this morning's paper, and none of this makes sense! Who are you?"

"It's not important."

"I can't come for someone whose name I don't know. Mental block."

That wasn't the only thing that would mentally block her from orgasm, but she had a feeling he was one stubborn man who would insist on finding that out for himself, no matter what.

The intruder paused. "Thorn."

She frowned. "Is that a first name or a last?"

"What do you need, my full name, social security number and blood type? This is simple—you either tell me where Curtis is or…I make you come and then you tell me."

Brenna sighed. "I swear, I don't know anything."

"We've been over this, babe. Besides…" He dedicated both hands to touching her breasts and toying with her nipples. "I'm enjoying the hell out of this. Cam's hard-on after his visit here makes a shitload of sense."

It shouldn't matter if she'd made the detective hard. He

was potentially the enemy and she wasn't likely to see too much of him in the future. But knowing she got to him…well, it did something for her feminine pride. Detective Martinez was a major hottie.

Then again, from what she could see of her intruder, Thorn was easy on the eyes too.

"I've got one myself," he added.

Oh, hell. Like she needed to know that he had an erection. A curl of thrill cut through her belly. Stupid…but it wasn't like she had a lot of control over the sensation.

"And I'm dying to know what you've got down south," he murmured in the dark.

Before she could protest, Thorn jerked the sheet away from her waist, past her hips, down her legs, then he ripped away the wisp of lace around her hips. Thanks to her bound and spread ankles, he had instant access to everything.

Thorn didn't hesitate, didn't work up to his next touch. He cupped the mound of her sex, fingers dipping just inside her lips to test. He slid right over slick, sensitive tissues, his fingers covering the quivering button of her clit.

He flashed her another smile in the dark. "Wet and bare, my favorite kind of pussy. It's going to be my pleasure to find out how many ways I can make you come."

"I don't think…"

He circled his fingers over her clit and bent to take that sore nipple in his mouth. At that point, thinking wasn't happening. She bucked and arched as sensation tore through her. A burning ache broiled between her legs. A line of tingles zinged between her nipple and her clit.

Oh…wow. This guy was good.

He moved his mouth to her other nipple, and let his teeth gently scrape her flesh. The connection between her nipple and parts south only increased. She shifted restlessly. So he wasn't just good, but *really* good.

Then he shocked her with a long, strong sucking of the nipple. She didn't want to respond to Thorn; he was a stranger in the dark, sweetly tormenting her for information she didn't have. She had nothing to give him, either in 411 or in orgasm. But logic wasn't stopping her body from arching to give more of herself and get closer to this man.

He lifted his hand from her sex and wrapped his left arm around her, securing his strapping forearm in the arch of her back to keep her lifted to his mouth. The hot, bare flesh of his chest and abdomen licked fire across the skin of her torso. Being closer to him was somehow more exciting than having his fingers on her clit. It felt more...personal. He felt more like a lover. A dangerous sensation, but Thorn was so solid all around her. Unlike all the guys in high school, his touch told her he was committed to giving her orgasm, not getting a ten-minute lay at a drunken party.

When he lifted his mouth from her nipple and moved it up her body, he nuzzled her neck, his hot breaths skittering across her sensitive skin. Goose pimples broke out. He nipped at her lobe and she gasped, but he quickly swallowed that sound with a demanding kiss.

He drove deep past her lips, sweeping inside as if he couldn't wait another minute to taste all of her mouth. Immediately, he proved that he hadn't had a drop of alcohol, unlike the guys in her past. All she tasted was spicy, aroused male.

Brenna didn't have to ask what he wanted, his desire to conquer her was all there in his groan, in his kiss. He challenged her with every thrust of his tongue, every frenzied sweep of his lips over hers. He was like a race car, built for speed and flash. If she let this go on, he'd dominate and do whatever necessary to ensure her compliance. Oh damn. The thought aroused her.

No, no, no!

He'd broken into Curtis' bungalow either to coerce information out of her or get laid. Neither motives were particularly sterling. She needed to tell him to get lost, go to hell and never come back.

Then he climbed up on the bed, between her legs, tore his vest off, and with a whispered, "Fuck, yeah," leaned over her body.

He fit his mouth right over her sex, his tongue swiping across her clit, providing maximum devastation.

Her cry filled the room as he swooped in for seconds, then thirds, then got really comfortable, as if he planned to stay for a while.

Without thinking, Brenna tried to raise her hands to tangle in that long golden mane. The cuffs stopped her short.

"Feel those cuffs," he whispered against her slick flesh. "I've got you just where I need you. God, you taste sweet. And those cuffs are going to keep you there until I've tasted every drop of cream this sweet pussy has to offer."

"This is insane." Her voice shook both with lingering fear and rising passion.

"This is hot."

He pushed her thighs a little wider, urging her to bend her knees and flare them out. The ties around her ankles stopped her eventually, but he opened her enough to dive deeper into her…and make her feel even more vulnerable than before.

Thorn didn't waste time getting back down to it. He struck quick and fast, with destructive results. Her resistance began to melt under the onslaught of his determined mouth. A swipe of his tongue before he sucked her whole clit into his mouth. Then—oh, God—he plunged a pair of fingers into her.

Her hips lifted, and she offered herself to him like a sacrifice.

Without hesitation, he took it.

The burn between her legs shimmered and grew, streaking up her belly, down her thighs. She began to tremble.

And Thorn showed no mercy—and no sign of letting up anytime soon.

But eventually he would let up. He would leave her. Every man did. Then...what? She would have given a part of herself to a man who didn't know her, wouldn't be there for her in the future. Did he even know her name? Could she pick him out in a crowd?

The thoughts ripped through her, leaving ugly shock in their wake. She was naked with and responding to a man who knew absolutely nothing about her and cared even less.

The fact she couldn't feel him anywhere on her body except between the legs all but shouted that she was just a pussy to him. She'd almost been more aroused by feeling his bare chest against hers, heart to heart, his mouth demanding a response from her. Without that...well, his touch felt more like a sensual attack than a shared pleasure.

Brenna sank back to the mattress, tensing, doing everything to close her legs against his determined mouth.

Thorn lifted his head to glare at her. "What the hell? Relax."

She shook her head. "I don't relax with men."

He quirked a golden brow. "With women?"

"Oh my...no!"

"Just checking. You one of those women who needs cock to get off?" He sat up and unsnapped the waistband of his leather pants. Then he reached for the zipper.

"Stop! I'm not the kind of woman to get off for a total stranger. Can we have a little light here? The dark is too...intimate, and I barely know you."

"I had my mouth on your pussy. If that's not getting to know you, what is?"

"A hit and run."

"Fuck," he muttered, then reached across her body to the lamp on the nightstand. Quickly, he flicked it on then leaned

47

over her body again.

Brenna took one look, and sucked in a stunned breath. Gorgeous, almost exotic in a Norse kind of way. He looked like she imagined a Scandinavian god would—but with leather and tats. Sun-kissed skin only accentuated the harsh slashes of cheekbone dominating each side of his face. And his ice-blue eyes left her speechless. Beautiful...and emotionally lifeless. He could be a seducer or a killer without much deliberation or remorse.

She began to shake.

"I'm sure you can find plenty of women who get into anonymous sex. I'm not one of them. I swear I've told you everything I know about Curtis Lawton. I don't know him well. I've seen him a handful of times in my whole life," she said truthfully. "Just...go."

Thorn said nothing for long moment. But those stunning eyes, they told her he was thinking hard and fast. She suspected very little got past this man.

"Curtis fuck you?"

"No. Never."

He paused again, then finally said, "You frigid?"

Brenna winced. God, she hated that word. It implied that a woman was somehow irreparably broken.

Well, aren't you?

"That's none of your business."

He stabbed his fists on his hips. "Since I'm the man in bed with you, baby, I beg to differ."

"My name is not baby!" Brenna bucked against her bonds. "Or honey or babe or—"

"Whatever. Does it matter? It's just a figure to speech."

She wanted to slap the man. "No, it's something you say when you don't know or can't remember a woman's name, isn't it?"

He didn't reply for a long moment. He didn't avoid her

stare or look contrite—he was too full of macho bullshit for that—but something told her she was right.

"You might be gorgeous and have the oral prowess of a god, but you've got the sensitivity of a doorknob."

Thorn smiled. "An oral god, huh?"

"You are totally missing the point. A woman can't relax for a man who doesn't know her name and doesn't care that he doesn't know. She wants to be cared for, cared about, feel that she—"

"Some women just want the orgasm, *baby*. I find plenty who are more than willing to forego the touchy-feely shit in favor of a really good fuck. So all your little speech tells me is that you're Cinderella waiting for Prince Charming." He rolled his eyes. "This ain't my department."

Before Brenna could question what that meant, Thorn climbed off the bed, grabbed the cell phone at his waist and stalked out of the bedroom.

* * * * *

Fuck.

"That went fabulously," Thorn muttered to himself, stabbing numbers into the keypad of his cell phone.

He was hard as hell and in over his head. Normally, a woman with her problems, suggesting he learn to be sensitive? He'd be gone—in a hurry. But this one...no. Not yet, anyway. She'd challenged him, and he planned to deliver.

The way she smelled aroused the fuck out of him. That lily-fair skin contrasted with her honey-brown hair. It fell in waves to her waist and framed her small, curved body. The effect made her look like a some kind of fairy, fragile, sensual, mysterious. Not his usual type—he liked women who looked like they loved sex. The loud, obvious ones. But this woman had great tits and hips, both of which he adored. The taste of her bare pussy on his tongue drove him wild. The thought of fucking her sent his hormones into overdrive. He had to, at

49

least once. But it was clear he was going to need reinforcements to do that.

On the fourth ring, he heard a froggy-groggy, "Hello?"

Thorn paused. "You sleeping or fucking?"

"Thorn?"

"No, it's the Tooth Fairy."

"Whaddya want. I'm sleeping."

"Get your ass over here."

"It's…" Thorn heard some scrambling on the other end of the phone, "one fifty-four in the morning. What's up?"

"I need your help."

Cameron sighed. "Where are you?"

"Curtis' bungalow in the Foothills."

"You're there with Brenna?"

Brenna. So that was her name. It was pretty, like her. It fit. When he came deep inside her, it would roll off his tongue.

"Yeah."

"Do I want to know why you're there with her in the middle of the night?"

"Probably not, since I tied her down to the bed and stripped her bare against her will. So you'd better come stop me, Detective."

With a chuckle, Thorn hung up. That would get Saint Cameron over here in a hurry. And since he already lived on the north side of town, he'd be here quick.

Goody, the night was just getting started.

Chapter Four

ဆ

Cameron pounded on the door to Curtis' love shack. The unseasonably crisp fall wind whipped under the shirt he hadn't bothered to button and around the bare toes he'd shoved into sandals as he'd grabbed his keys and run out the door.

What the hell was Thorn up to?

After a long minute, the door opened. Cameron fought the wind to shove his hair out of his face and behind his neck. He really meant to have it cut and kept forgetting.

There stood Thorn with a tight smile, an impatient tapping of his palm against his thigh...and a hard-on that strained his leathers.

So Brenna had the same effect on Thorn. Cameron didn't know whether to laugh or pity the poor bastard.

"What do you mean you tied her up and stripped her down against her will?" he asked, barging his way inside.

"Just what I said. We made a deal—if I could make her come, she would tell me everything she knows."

Not knowing Brenna well, Cameron couldn't say for sure that Thorn was lying, but it sounded fishy.

"If you couldn't?"

"I'd leave her alone. But we both know I can't do that until we have some info on Curtis. We have to run the bastard down, and Brenna is our only lead."

With the trial in five days? Yeah, he was feeling the heat. Curtis had skipped town and knew a thousand scumbags who would provide him a million places to hide. He didn't want to play hardball with Brenna. Playing Thorn's game, whatever it was, might cost him his badge. But when he looked into the faces of the slavers' victims—old men and women forced to labor in fields or over sewing machines until they dropped, or young boys and girls stripped of their innocence in cruel brothels catering to the depraved—he was determined to give this case his all. Husbands and wives, parents and children, had all been separated, their lives forever changed. The American dream shattered because of greedy pricks like Lawton and his boss, Julio Marco.

Lawton had agreed to turn evidence for the state. The Feds wouldn't comment on the condition of their case, so Cam wasn't about to leave any stone unturned, just in case they had a big bag of nothing. His job was to make sure the state's case stuck like Superglue. That meant hunting down Lawton. Brenna was his only hope at this point.

It sucked when his job played hell with his ethics.

"Agreed," Cam told Thorn reluctantly. "What do you have so far?"

"Shit. Nothing about Lawton. She keeps swearing she knows nothing."

"You're not buying it?"

"Why would Lawton let some woman he barely knows and wasn't fucking stay in his little mountain hideaway?"

"He wouldn't." Cameron sighed. "Anything else?"

"About her body, plenty. She's a hot little piece with a bare pussy that tastes like ambrosia. But something's wrong, man. She doesn't just come when stimulated like other women. She's looking for someone *sensitive*. That's where you come in."

Cameron frowned as a picture of Thorn's head between Brenna's slender thighs popped into his head. He wished he could say it disturbed him, but damn it, no. It aroused him. He'd never been the voyeur type and was never sexually fixated during cases. It had to stop.

"You think I'm going to arouse information out of her?"

he asked.

"Yeah, do that sensitive shit you do best, she'll fold like a lawn chair and start singing like a good churchgoer on Sunday."

"Did you try straightforward questioning, without the fondling?"

Thorn nodded. "I wasn't getting anything out of her. Then I got...distracted. Besides, interrogation isn't my thing. I cuff 'em and bring 'em in. I leave all that evidence and confession stuff to you cop types."

Cameron shook his head. Yes, Thorn's ADD impatience would be an impediment to good investigation. His insistence on living his life through his dick would be a real issue when it came to questioning beautiful women like Brenna.

"All right, let me see her. I'm not touching her to get information out of her, Thorn. Sex isn't a bet or a game or a deal. It's people sharing their bodies and emotions, being close to each other—"

"Oh, vomit. You two are going to get along great."

Thorn stomped off, deeper into the dark house. At least he'd had the foresight not to flip on lights, just in case one of Julio Marco's hit men was looking for an easy target.

Down an adobe-tiled path that bisected the kitchen and family room area, Cameron followed Thorn. A wall signaled a dead end, then Thorn turned left and opened the door.

Soft yellow light glowed in every corner of the room, falling over Brenna's bound, naked body, exposing every inch he'd been imagining since meeting her. Immediately, the nagging erection he'd been trying to shake for the last fifteen hours returned with a vengeance.

Damn. He had to get his mind off his cock, and what he'd love to do with it to Brenna.

"Too much light in here. If our friend Julio has one of his assassins—"

53

"Covered," Thorn cut in, pointing to the floor-to-ceiling windows to his right that overlooked the backyard. "Metal shutters cover the windows. No light in or out."

Good. One less thing to worry about. Except now he had nothing to focus on except Brenna Sheridan, her naked body and how badly he wanted to be inside her.

"Detective," she cried. "He broke in, tied me up in my sleep and fondled me without my permission."

"Not exactly true. I used the key under the flower pot on the front porch to let myself in, and I touched you with your permission—more or less. I asked you if you'd tell me what I wanted to know if I made you come, and you said yes."

"I didn't mean it."

"How was I supposed to know that? You were wet as hell when I touched you. As far as I'm concerned our bargain still stands."

"Even if it did," Brenna argued. "You didn't make me come."

Thorn flushed red. "I came damn close. Besides, you didn't specify that I personally had to make you come, just that I had to make sure it happened. Cam will take care of the technicalities."

Cam sighed and opened his mouth to refute Thorn.

Brenna shot back, "He can't make me come, either."

Normally, Cameron would let such a comment slide off his back. He didn't have the chest-beating, macho caveman instincts Thorn possessed. But somehow, Brenna's bald statement riled him a touch.

"Actually, I think, under normal circumstances, I could. I'm a patient man willing to take the time to discover what my partner needs during sex." He cocked his head and stared at Brenna. An odd sort of longing crossed her face. He remembered the night by the pool, watching her frustrated attempt to orgasm. "But what you're talking about is deeper, right?" He crossed the room to sit on the bed beside her.

"Have you ever had an orgasm?"

Brenna flushed twenty shades of red then turned away.

He took that to mean no.

An orgasm deficit to most would not be a huge tragedy. Through most of high school and college, Cameron had gone without. Too many people underfoot for self-pleasure. In his mostly white school, too many folks had been unwilling to get naked with someone half Apache, half Hispanic. In Arizona, that century-and-a-half-year-old prejudice against Indians and Mexicans still quietly lived on in more than a handful of people.

But Brenna... Her deficit wasn't a mere case of going without. It was an inability, her shamed expression told him. And Cameron ached for her. What would it be like to be an adult and not know the joy of sexual satisfaction?

Tragedy.

"See? She's frigid," Thorn mouthed off.

Cameron whirled on him. "Has anyone ever told you what an enormous prick you are?"

Thorn grinned. "No, but I hear frequently what an enormous prick I have."

Cameron rolled his eyes then turned back to Brenna. "Ignore him. When the phrase son of a bitch was coined, they had Thorn in mind."

"You're not much better. Pinching me so hard it brought tears to my eyes."

So he had. Totally unlike him. This stupid plot of Thorn's wasn't getting them anywhere, but he may be onto something.

"Key." He held out his palm to Thorn.

"Ah, shit. Man, you're going to uncuff her? She looks hot, bound and ready."

She did. No refuting that. But Thorn couldn't see the long-term benefit of uncuffing Brenna beyond the short-term benefit the view provided his dick.

"I'd hate to have to arrest you. You'd have to call your brother to bail you out."

"Oh, hell no!" With another curse, Thorn slapped the key in Cam's palm. "You ruin all the fun, you know that?"

"I'm the original party pooper."

With a quick turn of his wrist and a few tugs, Brenna's wrists were free. He untied her ankles. Just as she would have leapt from the bed and reached for the robe on the floor beside it, Cameron placed a palm between her bare collarbones.

"Not just yet." Once he had her pinned to the bed, he said, "I am sincerely sorry that no man has taken the time or care with you to give you the pleasure you deserve. I'm sorry you have yet to figure out how to bring yourself to orgasm." He brushed a stray curl from her cheek. "I know it must bother you. You must feel somewhat left out and…defective."

Tears flooded Brenna's eyes, and Cameron sucked in a shocked breath. He'd hoped that he was close to the truth, but hadn't imagined that he was dead on. Her tears and pained expression said, however, that he was.

"It's okay," he whispered. "You're not. It's wrong for you to go on suffering needlessly. We will help you discover what you need to find fulfillment, if that's what you want. But…" Cameron sighed, hating what he had to say next. "Thorn is right. We need your help in return. Lawton worked with a man named Julio Marco and others to traffic humans across the border and sell them into slavery. I was Lawton's arresting officer. Thorn is his bail bondsman. We need Lawton to live up to his word to turn evidence for the state so the victims can have justice. He must come in and provide the testimony he promised. You're our only hope of finding him."

Brenna blinked. Tears ran down the sides of her face. Cameron hurt for her. She was clearly confused, didn't know who to trust or what to do. He understood.

Cameron thumbed her tears away. "I would never want to hurt you. I believe we can help you. In return, I hope you're willing to help us." He leaned down and placed a gossamer kiss across her trembling lips. "Will you?"

Sincerity. It poured from the detective's soulful dark eyes. That, and compassion. He really understood on some level, especially the feeling defective part.

Under the guise of closing her eyes, she stole a quick glance. He was really perfect. How could he imagine for an instant that he was defective? Or was his flaw hidden on the inside, like hers?

What should she do? Logic shouted at her to tell them both to go to hell. Orgasms for information. Crazy! Cameron might look empathetic, but she didn't know him well at all. And Thorn...he'd been treating her like a piece of ass all night.

On the other hand, why had she traveled from Texas to Tucson? It wasn't to patch things up with Curtis precisely. Their relationship was likely beyond redemption, and she'd begun to realize that he was more than happy with the status quo. But she had come here to find some peace and closure about this part of her life, in the hopes that, when she met a great guy, she could be "normal" and have a decent sex life with him. Her inability to orgasm had already cost her one meaningful relationship. It was only a matter of time before it cost her more. Lord knew her self-confidence had already taken a beating.

In a way, it was a plus that Thorn and Cameron were relative strangers. If she tried three in a bed with any of the local yokels back in Muenster, her reputation would be ruined. Didn't matter that it was the twenty-first century, small towns were timeless when it came to scandal.

Glancing up again, she caught Thorn's expression—and frowned. He actually looked somewhere between curious and confused. That was a whole lot better than his confident jackass expression, the one that made her certain that Thorn thought all he had to do was show her his dick and her problems would be solved.

Now, he watched the way Cameron caressed her cheek. When his blue-blue gaze connected with hers, it was like a punch to the stomach, taking the breath right out of her.

"Brenna, I know you don't have any reason to agree, other than the fact we could help each other. I'd help you, even if I didn't need the information. That much confusion and pain just doesn't belong on such a beautiful face."

Unless the detective dabbled in acting, he meant those words. Wow… Why say no? They were both gorgeous, and having two men at once sounded like a most arousing fantasy. Maybe they could help her solve her problem. Yes, she knew she was probably grasping at straws, but she already had been when she traveled out here, hoping that something in her interaction with Curtis would help heal her. Maybe what she needed was hands-on therapy. She could do worse than two gorgeous hunks devoted to helping her achieve orgasm.

Why are you hesitating? a voice inside her asked.

Good question.

"A-all right. But there are a few rules."

Cameron smiled softly. "Name them."

Brenna shot a glare at Thorn. "No tying me down without my permission."

Thorn growled but Cameron grabbed him by the shoulder and squeezed. Hard. The bounty hunter winced.

"Goddamn you, Cameron. You know I got shot there a few months ago," he cursed, pulling away.

"Just so we understand each other. Brenna is laying out boundaries, and we're agreeing."

"She wants to take all the fucking fun out of everything…but whatever."

Cam rolled his eyes as Thorn rolled his shoulder with a glare. Then he turned back to Brenna. "What else?"

"Condoms all around."

"Of course," Cameron soothed.

"No shit. Like I'd want to be bareback wherever Dudley Do-Right has been."

With an inky brow raised, Cam turned to Thorn. "You're the one with the drive-through sex life. I worry about where you've been."

"This is such fucking—"

"Rule three—you two stop fighting. I'll never relax enough to orgasm if I have to listen to you two quibble like old ladies."

They turned to her, wearing almost identical puzzled expressions. Brenna barely held in a laugh.

"Old ladies?" they challenged in unison.

She merely nodded. "Last, it stops when I say so."

Cameron nodded, and beside him, Thorn scoffed. "Look, I may be a prick but stop means stop. I'm not into rape."

Handy information. Brenna had wondered if Thorn had *any* morals. "Good. We're agreed then."

"Absolutely."

"Hell, yeah," Thorn added.

"I'd like to make a request," Cameron said. At Brenna's nod, he continued on. "If either of us does anything you dislike, you tell us immediately. We don't want you gritting your teeth through any of this."

"I will," Brenna vowed. "Thank you for being so sensitive."

"That's Saint Cam. While we're being all honest with our feelings and shit," Thorn began, "I have a request too. You're naked," he said to Brenna. "Whenever and wherever I want you, you're naked and ready. Is that clear?"

Her heart jumped, and Brenna felt her breath tremble accordingly. Cameron didn't miss a single thing, with his gaze wrapped all over her. Was he looking for her acceptance? Her weaknesses? He studied her so intently… Wondering how a grown woman could make it to twenty-six years old without so much as a single contraction of her womb, no doubt. God, what a wretchedly embarrassing feeling.

"I'm not a bimbo who will pretend to come to preserve your precious ego. Do *not* treat me like a piece of ass. I won't be one for you or anyone."

Thorn hesitated then looked her over thoroughly. The man had eyes. No doubt, he was seeing the tears on her face, the vulnerability in her expression she knew was there and couldn't hide.

"Okay," he said, his voice surprisingly gentle. "But I want you naked."

"Fine," she relented.

"It's settled," Cameron cut in. "Brenna, you'll be naked or mostly so. Thorn will not behave like an asshole. At least beyond what's natural and can't be helped."

"Funny." Thorn rolled his eyes.

"Now what?" Brenna asked breathlessly.

Her heart was beating...beating. Was she really going to do this? In a word, yes. She had no reason not to, other than the fact they were relative strangers. But they were also attractive, knew about her problem and didn't think she was a freak—a huge plus. She knew from their occupations and the instinct in her gut that they wouldn't hurt her. And they had aroused her more than any other men in her life. Honestly, if she wanted to figure out the key to having a normal sex life, it just wasn't going to get much better than this.

"I have an idea, if you'll give it a chance," Cam said.

She shrugged. "I don't have any ideas of my own."

"I have to be honest. Whatever happens, we need information about Curtis by sunrise. I can't let all those victims and their families down. I just can't."

And she supposed Thorn had ponied up a pretty penny to get Curtis out of jail. No doubt, he wanted it back.

"Of course." She took a deep breath and tried to shoot them a chipper smile.

Inside, she felt anything but. What if this, like everything else, failed? She'd tried every technique, sex toy, fantasy, erotic book. She'd even gone to Dallas and hired an "escort" once. Nothing. If all that stuff designed for good sex had failed, why would a detective and a bail bondsman succeed?

"Whatever is running through your head, stop now," Cameron advised, his tone a gentle command. "You're sabotaging yourself before we've even started."

He was right. She had to put all the worries about being defective and the doubts about this plan out of her mind. She couldn't dwell on tomorrow. Right now was much more crucial.

"What's your idea?"

"Thorn will arouse you—at my direction. I'll be watching to see what pleases you, what makes you tense. What makes you melt with pleasure and what makes you freeze. I'll adjust him accordingly."

"Dude," Thorn directed at Cam, who looked braced for an argument. Instead, the bounty hunter clapped him on the shoulder. "That's a sweet idea. I get all the fun, and you merely get to think about it." He turned to her, and Brenna found herself falling into blue eyes that were suddenly, surprisingly alive. "All the women call him 'patient' and 'perceptive". If anyone will figure out how to make this work, it's Cam."

Thorn's little speech, odd as it was, worked. It wasn't a stretch to see Cam as patient and perceptive. Maybe with his thoughts on the task and Thorn's fingers—or whatever else—doing the walking, that miraculous big 'O' would finally happen for her.

"O-okay."

"Good. Thorn, kiss her. Like you mean it. Like you never want to stop."

"That's not hard. I didn't want to stop earlier."

Brenna blushed as Thorn stalked toward the bed and lowered himself on the opposite side. He crawled across the mattress, then over her, forcing her back against the cool sheet. He hovered above her like a conquering predator, ruthless smile and all.

He both scared and excited her. She'd never known that feeling before Thorn, but she already knew the achy, panicky feeling wasn't going to be conducive to relaxation and sexual satisfaction.

"Wait," she breathed.

Above her, Thorn's smile fell. How many times had she seen confusion or disappointment on a man's face? Too many, and to know she might only be repeating the pattern... Maybe this wasn't such a good idea after all.

"What is it?" Cameron asked.

She faced him with fresh tears in her eyes. "This isn't going to work. Never mind. I'll tell you what I know about Curtis. It's very little and I doubt it will help but—"

"Why do you think this won't work?"

Sighing, Brenna stared at Cameron, hyperaware of Thorn braced over her. "Did you hear me? I'll tell you what I know."

"I know you will. But I won't just abandon you. You're willing to give us something we need. We're willing to give you the same."

They wouldn't abandon her. Or rather Cameron wouldn't. But a glance at Thorn's face said he was on Cam's bandwagon. The smile was gone, replaced by...concern? Not exactly. Pity? Maybe, and that shamed her. But still, his face said something else she couldn't pinpoint.

"Yeah," he murmured. "I might bitch and moan about the fact we're not fucking yet, but I'm not going to just leave you like this. You're stuck with me, *Brenna*."

So Thorn did know her name...

But why were they being so insistent about helping her? "Guys, I'm not a good lay."

"Let us be the judge. You tell me what was stopping you before Thorn kissed you and we'll deal with it."

Brenna closed her eyes. Here she wanted to change her life, but she was too afraid. She was going to have to choose. Doing the same old things was going to get her the same old results. Ignoring it, masturbating, buying sex toys, living a fantasy life—none of that was going to get her where she wanted to go.

Maybe brutal honesty would.

She swallowed. "Thorn, the way you smiled at me just before you were going to kiss me. It was like a...pirate."

Total confusion crossed his chiseled face. "Pirate? Like...grrr, mateys?"

"I'm saying it wrong. I felt like something you wanted to plunder purely for your own pleasure, not like something that meant anything to you. I don't expect to mean anything to you after an hour, it's just...I can't relax if I'm feeling like I'll be used and left."

"We're not leaving," Cameron assured.

Thorn sat back on his haunches. "Too strong, huh? I guess I only know about the type of female who likes to put out and get cock in return. We never have expectations between us. I'm not sure how else to act."

Brenna sat up, never taking her eyes off Thorn. That was the most he'd ever said to her—and the most honest. And it had pained him to say it.

"You never stay past morning?"

He scoffed. "I never stay *until* morning. But if that's what you need, I will."

"Because you feel sorry for me?" Oh God, if he did, someone open a huge hole in the floor and let her crawl inside.

"I do but that's not why. The last hour or so have proved

63

to me that you're not Lawton's fuck. He couldn't catch a woman this...real. Hell, I never have." Thorn heaved a sigh. "As you said earlier, you're not a bimbo. And I'm so out of my league. I'll leave you to Cameron."

Thorn rose to leave the bed. Brenna reached out and curled her hand around his biceps. It was like cradling living, breathing stone in her palm. Cameron grabbed his wrist.

"Stay," they both said.

"I'm not suited to this kind of gig. She wants something emotional, man. You know that's not me," he said to Cameron.

Cam shrugged. "So it will be a first for all of us. Brenna is going to have an orgasm and you're going to get in touch with your sensitive side."

"You're assuming I have one."

"Underneath all that badass? I think you do."

"I won't think you're less macho if I see it," Brenna promised.

"What's your first in all this?" Thorn asked Cameron.

"I've never watched people have sex or had anyone watch me have it."

"It can be one hell of a kick." Thorn flashed him a grin.

"Figures you'd know. I can't have that experience if you leave."

"You're going to pin this shit on me?"

"Yep." Cam nodded.

"You know that's unfair."

Cam shrugged. "It doesn't change a damn thing."

"Fuck," Thorn whispered. "This is getting awfully touchy-feely."

Cameron slanted him a calculating glance. "You really going to walk away from the chance to be with Brenna? Look at her."

Three words, and she was acutely self-conscious of her

nudity under the golden glow of the lamp. Both men turned their gazes to her, and she felt their stares crawl up her legs, caress her belly, linger on her breasts. She got wet all over again, even as she brought her hands and knees up to cover herself.

Without exchanging a word, Thorn grabbed her wrist and leg on one side of her body. Cameron took hold of the other.

"No hiding," Cam whispered. "Please."

"You said naked and available," Thorn reminded. "If I'm going to endure Dr. Phil Frankenstein here," he nodded at Cam, "throw me a bone."

She had given him her word. But this was all just so weird.

"Let's start with a kiss," the detective suggested. "Nothing big, no pressure. You like to kiss?"

"I love it," she admitted.

"Good. If you don't want more after that, we'll talk about it,"

"But it wasn't working when Thorn tried. I froze up."

"All I have for my effort is blue balls," Thorn groused.

"Do you want me to try?" Cam offered.

"Why the hell not, Boy Scout? Show me how it's done."

She shot Thorn a glare then turned to Cameron. "Please."

Leaning closer, Cam scooted beside her. Caressing her face, he tucked her silky hair behind her ear and murmured, "Stop me if you need to."

Brenna nodded, until Cameron took hold of the back of her neck. Gently, but she felt his fingers there all the same. A zip and sizzle made their way across her skin, down her spine.

"You're shaking," he whispered.

"You get to me," she admitted.

"That's what I like to hear."

Slowly, Cameron leaned in. Brenna hesitated, then began

to meet him. He watched her all the way with those expressive eyes. His chiseled cheekbones looked exotic, rather than harsh. And his mouth…tender and capable of granting the sweetest pleasure.

In that moment, she yearned for everything else possible from him.

Finally, he lips brushed hers, a barely there thing, but electric just the same. She felt the impact of his gentleness in every corner of her body. Then he eased away.

Brenna pursued, crushing her mouth against his. On her neck, his fingers tightened. He slanted his head again, finding the perfect angle until their lips fit together naturally, as if they were made that way, halves of the same whole. She sighed, and he pressed to her, tangling her top lip between his then shifting to the bottom. Another brush of lips, followed by a lingering kiss on her jaw, her neck, and she moaned.

He moved in for the kill then, urging her willing lips apart with his own. Plunging deep inside, he took her by storm. The male tang of him tantalized her tongue. The sensual dance of their mouths mesmerized her. Deep and seemingly endless, the kiss intoxicated. Brenna wanted to melt against him and beg him to do it forever.

Cameron pulled back, and with a last soft press of lips, disengaged. "What you had in mind?"

God, she still felt drunk off him. Her lashes fluttered open, and she touched a hand to her tingling lips. "Yes."

"Fuck, that was hot," Thorn whispered. "You didn't do anything but kiss her."

Shaking his head, he said to the bounty hunter, "Right. A kiss isn't always a prelude to getting down and dirty. Sometimes, it just…is, all on its own."

He'd said that perfectly. Brenna sighed and sidled up to Cameron. Maybe she could persuade him to do it again.

"Holy shit. I never tried that route. I thought it was just for chick flicks and Hallmark cards."

Thorn hesitated, looked between Cameron and her then settled on her face. Her mouth. Their gazes connected with a *bam*, like an earthquake rattled through her. She wasn't sure she liked or trusted him. What was it about him that kept her responding?

"I wanna kiss you again."

Brenna knew just from the way he said the words that there'd be no more modern pirate chasing his booty call.

Suddenly, she was intensely curious to see what Thorn was like under all that macho bluster. "Okay."

Cameron's hand had settled gently behind her neck, acting as both support and guide. Thorn thrust his fingers into her hair until he cradled the crown in his palm. Instead of sitting beside her and meeting her face to face, he rose up over her, tilted her head back, raising her lips up to his. His other hand cupped her jaw. And still, he never took his eyes off her.

Thorn hesitated, thumb caressing her cheek. "I want to do this right."

"You're doing good so far," she assured, anticipation making her voice high and thin.

He bent down, leaned in, keeping her stare as he drew closer…closer. Finally, he closed his eyes, then touched his lips to hers. Soft. There, but not dominating like before.

For a long moment, he didn't move, didn't seek to deepen the kiss. Didn't do anything.

Except begin to shake.

She felt the tremor against her lips first. Tentatively, Brenna touched his shoulder. He shook there too. His abs rippled under her fingers, as well. Raising her hand from his shoulder to his back, she realized he was trembling all over.

Brenna moved to retreat, but Thorn fisted his hand in her hair and plunged into her mouth. But it wasn't cocky authority she tasted in his kiss this time. It was desperation.

It shocked her from head to toe. She gripped him tighter

and opened to him. Immediately, she tasted need. *He* needed her?

At the moment, the reasons why didn't matter.

She rose up on her knees and met his reckless onslaught. Thorn grabbed her tighter in greedy acceptance, pulling her body against his. Though Brenna hadn't thought it possible, he deepened the kiss. Fast, a whirl of taste and touch, he swept through her mouth. Desire, heavy and warm, flashed in her belly. The ache Cameron had kindled to life swelled into a full-fledged burn.

Clutching him, Brenna moaned.

Beside them, Cameron rose, closed in, touched her arm. Was he concerned for her?

Or aroused by the sight of them?

If he noticed Cameron, Thorn ignored him, lowering the hand at her jaw to her shoulder, then down to cover her breast. His touch was firm but not harsh, and his fingers on her skin created electric tingles that shimmied through her body, awakening nerves she hadn't known she possessed.

Again, his mouth claimed hers, one hot stroke of his tongue after another, and Brenna fell into the taste of him, the heat of his touch. It was a delicious drowning, and it might kill her. Right now, she didn't care—as long as Thorn kept heaping the sensations on her.

And still, she felt Cameron's hand, now on her shoulder, acutely, burning her skin with the heat of his palm. The longer he lingered, the more she swore she could feel his desire.

Between the two of them, she was on fire.

Then Thorn took her nipple between his thumb and forefinger—and pinched.

"Ouch!" She pulled away from Thorn with an accusing stare.

"What the…?" He looked her over, his laser-blue gaze zeroing in on her breasts. "Oh, hell. You're sore. I forgot."

"You can't just pinch her," Cameron pointed out. "Don't squeeze her like your fingers are a pair of pliers."

"I didn't," Thorn defended. "That was you, and she's been sore ever since."

"Really?" Cameron turned to her.

Brenna nodded. "I'm fine. Just a little sensitive."

"I'm sorry," Cameron murmured. "I had to know about you and Curtis…"

He didn't finish the sentence but palmed her breast, caressing her nipple with a gentle thumb. Already hard, her nipple now stood up straight for him. His touch burned clear to her belly…and lower.

Thorn moaned, still kneeling inches from her, his hand wrapped around her neck, the other at her hip, anchoring her close to him. And, with burning hot eyes, he was watching Cameron touch her, soothing her with a slow, repentant caress.

With an audible swallow, Thorn demanded, "Kiss it and make it better."

Cameron's eyes flashed up to Thorn. Neither said anything for long moments. Did she want them both touching her at the same time? Would they?

God knew she'd never been more aroused in her life than she was now. Even the thought of having both men's hands on her was broiling her insides.

Something passed between the men, a look. An understanding?

Then Cameron turned his dark stare to her. It was a question, a silent one. He wouldn't proceed without some sign from her.

And somehow Brenna knew that speaking now would shatter the fragile situation. One wrong word or move, and someone would leave. Besides, what could she say that her body couldn't say for her?

Brenna arched into Cameron's hand and closed her eyes.

A moment later, warm lips pressed to the side of her breast. A soft brush of lips, a caress. Then he pursed his lips around her nipple. His soft tongue stroked her a moment later. And her head spun with amazing sensation. Desire flared hot in her belly, streaking fire through her, then centered lower, under her clit. She was burning up from the inside and she loved it. A moan slipped past her lips.

Thorn captured it with his mouth.

With a gasp, Brenna took in the fact both men were kissing some part of her.

Excitement danced in her belly, burning. They'd stoked a banked fire inside her, and now it was roaring.

After trailing kisses across her cheek, Thorn nipped at her lobe, then whispered, "You look hot with Cam sucking your nipple. You like it?"

"Yes," she blurted on a moan. "Yes."

"Want more?"

"Please."

Thorn cupped her other breast and teased the nipple with his thumb, watching every pull and pucker of Cameron's mouth. He was so gentle, it didn't hurt. Pleasure just washed over her. And knowing Thorn loved the sight of it somehow ramped her up higher.

"Cam," he murmured.

In response, he moaned, tugged gently on her nipple with his lips, laved one last time, then raised his gaze to her.

God, he pulled her in. His eyes were on fire, his cheeks flushed. She felt the heat radiating from him. Brenna glanced down at his jeans. No doubt about the state of his arousal.

"Cam?"

Taut and on edge, the detective cut his eyes over to Thorn. Quickly, his gaze dropped from Thorn's face, following the line of his arm down, down. Cameron's eyes flashed with something wild as he fixed on the sight of Thorn's hand palming her breast. Then Thorn lifted it up, offering it to Cam.

He didn't have to offer twice.

Brenna watched his dark head shift toward the other breast. He brushed a pair of kisses against the curve, then he captured the nipple deep in his mouth. Hot and oh-so capable, he made her moan once more.

She couldn't take her eyes off them, Thorn holding her breast in offering to Cam, him hungrily taking it. The visual alone was killer. The feeling of those fingers and lips together on her flesh... God, tingles ruthlessly beat at her. Her skin felt too tight. She was restless and plagued by a growing ache, now bigger than she was. Grabbing Thorn for another kiss would make her feel better...and worse. But she did it anyway.

The feel of his hair filtering through her fingers was surprisingly silky and she drew her mouth back to his. He didn't ask questions or resist but instead dived into her mouth like he was never going to get enough of her. Like he'd never leave her, as long as he was this addicted to her flavor.

And Cam...his mouth seemed permanently attached to her nipples, his teeth grazing the one he hadn't abused yesterday, sensitizing it until it stood erect so he could tongue it and make her even wetter than before. Make her feel like she was the only woman in his world.

With a last nip of his teeth on her lower lip, Thorn pulled back then slid his hand over her breast, breaking the suction of Cam's mouth.

Cam jerked his gaze up to his friend with a frown.

"Were you going to leave any for me?" Thorn challenged.

Chapter Five

ဢ

The words took a minute to sink in, it appeared. Cameron blinked then turned his gaze from Thorn, over to her. He was panting, his chest, smooth and built and bronze, heaved up and down quickly. A moment later, Brenna realized he wasn't the only one breathing hard. And the longer he looked at her, the less she could seem to draw a decent breath.

"Are you okay with this? I want you to be comfortable and happy—"

"Try ecstatic. Please, kiss me," she implored.

Cameron didn't have to be asked twice.

As he lifted his head, angling his mouth closer to hers, Thorn began to descend. They met somewhere in the middle, and Cameron cautioned, "Gentle."

Thorn's hand on her hip tightened. "Got it, Saint Cam."

Thunder crossed the detective's face but Thorn had already blown the exchange off and headed south.

A moment later, Thorn's tongue curled around her nipple before he took the whole thing in his mouth, sucking as if he'd like to swallow it whole. He marked the other with his tongue a moment later, the sore one, with a gentle laving and a sweet suckle.

Brenna filtered her fingers deeper into Thorn's hair and moaned.

Cameron cupped her cheek in his hand. "I don't know why seeing his mouth at your breast is a turn-on, but..." He closed his eyes. "I don't recall ever being this aroused."

"Me, either."

"You know we won't leave you until you have what you

need."

She nodded. Because she did know it. For whatever reason, they were devoted to this cause and devoted to her. Something heavy and magical was swirling between them. Always, she knew before the sex even started that the man holding her and praising her body would leave her at some point, sooner rather than later. Some sense, deep in her bones, told her these two would be with her for a good long while, if only in spirit.

This wasn't lasting. She lived in Texas. In fact, her plane ticket was scheduled to take her back home in another week. But this connection between the three of them felt weirdly deep.

Brenna didn't fight it.

Drowning in the feel of Thorn worshipping her breasts and Cameron making love to her with his heady dark eyes, she whispered, "Kiss me."

Cam eagerly accepted her invitation.

This kiss was like his first…and it wasn't. No longer just a gentle caress of mouths, a soft melding of lips, now he added a sensual swipe of tongue that had her seeking him out, eagerly entwining with him then mewling for more.

Sensations bombarded her, saturating her completely. God, she felt dizzy and heavy and so hot—and she loved it.

Then Thorn caressed his way from her hip to her sex—and everything ramped up a notch. Unerringly, his fingers found her clit and toyed insistently with the little bundle. Arousal gripped tighter, choking whatever resistance she had left. He knew just how and where to touch her to completely devastate her senses.

Thorn lifted his head with a gasp. "Lay her back, get her horizontal. I gotta get my mouth on this pussy again."

Cameron braced a hand between her shoulder blades while Thorn guided her back at the hips. Brenna uncurled her legs so she was no longer kneeling. When her back met the mattress, Thorn dived between her legs, spreading them wider, and latched onto her with a ravenous impatience that made her shiver.

As she cried out, Brenna looked up at Cam with half-open lids. He loomed above her, caressed her cheek.

"You're flushed," he murmured, his gaze straying south. "Is Thorn making you feel good?"

Brenna couldn't find her voice. She nodded then moaned again when Thorn thrust two fingers inside her.

"You look so sexy," he went on, those watchful eyes of his ping-ponging between her eyes and Thorn latched onto her sex.

Cam's hands were in motion too. His fingertips danced across her collarbone, a glide of palms over her shoulder, a brush of thumbs over her nipples.

The stimulation was almost too much. Coupled with the eye candy overload of having them both in her bed, she almost couldn't process it. But she wanted more.

She reached up to Cam's shoulder, easing her fingers under the collar of his unbuttoned shirt, and slipped it down. He shrugged it off that one arm. Before he could remove it from the other, Brenna had already caressed it off, leaving him bare from the waist up.

"You sure?" he asked with a concerned frowned.

"I am when you kiss me."

Thankfully, he took the hint and took her mouth a heartbeat later. Urgent, passionate, possessive, his kiss amazed her, added to the overall body tingle Thorn was sparking inside her. Brenna clutched Cameron's bare shoulders and held him close. His hands continued to roam her face, her neck, her breasts. Soon, his mouth fell to her nipples to join in.

Brenna stared at the white ceiling, for once not trying to second-guess or process what was happening. She was just feeling, and it wasn't just the physical stuff. Oh, that was there, rising within her with all the subtlety of a jackhammer at 5 a.m. on a Sunday. But a lingering feeling that she was meant to be here with them gave her the courage to go on and believe that, this time, she wouldn't fail.

Sensations rose in waves. Heat rolled through her, making her feel weak and heavy and overloaded on pleasure. She clutched the sheets and realized that her whole body was shaking. Blood rushed between her legs. She could actually feel it, along with the growing pressure.

Thorn lifted his mouth from her, replacing his tongue with fingers that seemed to know the perfect spot. "She's getting close, man. Really close. I'm going to glove up."

Cameron gave him a distracted nod then wended his way down her body, brushing soft kisses across her belly, sweeping his palms over her hip, to her thigh. Planting his palm on the inside, he pushed her leg farther apart then repeated the process with the other. Brenna was tempted to tell him that she couldn't do the splits and didn't want to learn now…but then he placed soft kisses on her low abdomen and kept going down.

Oh dear God.

Cam's first pass through her wet, sensitive sex was an electric shock that caused her to gasp. The next was a pleasure bomb that detonated right where she needed it most and forced her to whimper.

She was so, so close now—closer to orgasm than she'd ever dreamed she could be.

"Cameron…" His name on her lips was both a cry and a plea for help.

He didn't answer, except to caress her hip with that broad, bronzed palm.

Brenna turned her head to find Thorn standing a few feet away, completely bare and stroking his erection. The sight made the pleasure pulse even deeper inside her. Wide shoulders tapered to narrow hips. A powerful chest matched the large cock he enveloped with his hand.

"You two look so fucking hot. Cam going to make you come?"

Brenna wanted to nod but was too tense. The sensations were right there, but something was still bound up inside her. She whimpered in answer.

Thorn crossed the room to Cam and knelt beside her thigh. Cam lifted his head and turned to Thorn, his stare heavy. Brenna watched Cam breathe hard, just inches from Thorn. In the room's muted lamp light, Cam's lips were shiny with her juice. Thorn's gaze dropped, and she bet he was noticing too.

A moment later, Thorn blinked and dropped his gaze, breaking the moment. "She having trouble?"

"She's almost there," Cam whispered. "A little more and…"

With a nod, Thorn stood and rolled on the condom. Then he climbed up on the bed on her right, then turned her on her left shoulder, facing Cam, who was climbing up on the bed, facing her.

Thorn lifted her top leg and eased it over his own. Brenna watched down her body as, dick in hand, Thorn fitted himself against her entrance.

"Talk to her, man," Thorn choked.

Cam nodded, his stare glued to the sight of Thorn's erection prodding her flesh.

And Thorn pushed up. Hard. To the hilt in one thrust.

A surprised cry slipped from Brenna. She felt beyond packed full. Her body stretched to accommodate him, but she felt his possession acutely, almost more than physically. It was like Thorn was in every corner of her, he was so deep.

"It's okay," Cam soothed, cradling her breast, thumbing her nipple. "We're going to make it good."

He put the exclamation point on his promise with a kiss that sent a hot shock through her body, tangling with the devastation of Thorn's intrusion. Gentle but insistent, full of reassurance — that's how Cam's kiss flowed through her.

Then Thorn started to move. Pound was more accurate. *Bam, bam, bam,* he drove inside her with shattering force. The headboard slammed the wall with every thrust, reverberating around the room.

Taking someone his size with such force after a long abstinence was nearly painful. She winced, and Cameron reached past her to grab Thorn's hip.

"Stop banging her like a goddamn drum. This is sex, not a heavy metal concert."

"Fuck you. I have no problems getting women off."

"You're hurting Brenna."

Behind her, Thorn stilled. "That true?"

"A little."

"Shit," he muttered. "I'm sorry. Slower?"

She nodded. "It's just been a while."

Thorn stilled. "Define a while."

"Nearly a year."

"No wonder you're having trouble, baby. Everything is rusty."

Cam rolled his eyes. "She's not a car."

"Shut up and let me drive," Thorn growled.

Though he nodded, Cam kept his hand on Thorn's hip, ready to act as a guide.

But Thorn delivered, easing straight up inside her at a pace like warmed honey, slow and flowing and breath-stealing.

Brenna grabbed the nearest anchor — Cameron. She clutched his shoulders and gasped. "Oh my... Yes."

"That's good?" he whispered against her mouth.

She nodded and whimpered. And when Thorn repeated the stroke, just as delicious and languorous as the first, Brenna lost her ability to form coherent words.

A third time had her digging her fingers into Cam's shoulders and mewling.

Then Cameron really joined in, capturing her mouth against his and sinking deep. He reached down and found her clit, toying lightly. God, she didn't know how much she could take. She had to explode. The pace of his oral invasion matched Thorn's sexual one, and the combination went straight to her libido.

She could smell them both, Thorn's sweat-damp body put off this musky scent that, as he pressed inside her again and draped his arm around her to fondle her breast—that unique tang on his skin was man and aggression and sex, wrapped in tempting spice. But in front of her, slowly enveloping her, was Cameron's complex scent. Powerful male for sure, rain-tinged, earthy. She smelled his want. Between the two of them, they produced an amazing olfactory high.

She shook with the intensity of her desire and kissed Cameron madly, so on the edge that coherent thought was completely beyond her—and she loved it.

As seconds slid into minutes, she stayed at the feverish point just shy of climax.

"Jesus, she's like a fist on my cock, man. She's tightening more with each second." He looked at Cameron then closed his eyes. "I don't know how much longer I can hold on."

With a nod, Cameron turned his attention to her. "Brenna, you know we want you. I know you feel the pleasure."

"I do," she whispered, then wailed, "It's right there! And I just can't…"

She started to cry, hot tears gouging her eyes.

"Can't what?" Cam brushed gentle kisses on her face.

Even Thorn dropped a tender brush of lips on her shoulder, skated a few across her neck. For the first time tonight, she felt truly cared about. Brenna had no doubt that was taking her farther down the road to orgasm than she'd been. Yes, it was taking her a while to arrive…and there was a good chance she'd never actually get there.

Maybe she was always going to have this block until she was convinced that her partner was with her to stay. Maybe she didn't need to talk to Curtis to understand that fear of ultimately being left just really kept her from sharing that most intimate part of herself.

She opened her mouth, wondered if she should call this whole orgasms-for-information deal off. It wasn't fair to them. They'd tried everything to help her. She'd offer up blowjobs, tell them what little she knew about Curtis then flee this place and return to Texas.

Before she could, Thorn murmured, "Baby, you want us to fill you up, front and back?"

It took Brenna a moment to realize what he meant. When his words finally unpuzzled themselves in her head, a hot spike of desire hit her right between the legs. Double penetration. One in her pussy, the other in her ass.

She didn't, for one moment, think it would make any difference in her orgasm quotient, but it was one helluva a fantasy. Brenna didn't delude herself, she was bad at sex. The whole orgasm thing always threw a dark cloud over her relationships. She ought to go home, adopt ten cats and settle in for spinsterhood. Before she did, however, she was going to take Thorn up on his offer and live out a dream.

After all, this chance was wasn't likely to come her way again.

"Please," she whimpered. "Now. Right now."

Thorn grabbed her chin and turned her head, tearing her away from Cam's kiss and covered her mouth with his own. He tasted like he fucked—aggressive, sure of himself, as if he loved it.

He lifted his head long moments later, and Brenna marveled that she could want two totally different men so much. They both made her body feel such arousal. Both were

Shayla Black

amazing in their own right—she could say that after sleeping with a string of losers in her younger days. These guys...they were damn good.

Thorn pillaged, making a commanding sweep through her mouth that matched the invasion of her body. The sensations excited her as much as they established Thorn's dominance. Her body hummed, her skin felt tight, and Cam continued to fondle her clit while he fixed his burning gaze on her.

Finally Thorn lifted his head and stared at Cam across the scant inches separating them all. Heavy breathing reigned.

"I gotta taste her pussy once more," Thorn groaned. "I can smell it, and she's driving me crazy."

Cameron lifted his fingers from her clit and extended them to Thorn's mouth.

Thorn reared back. "I'm not sucking your fingers."

"You are if you want a taste of her now. I've been waiting to be inside her, and I'm not in the mood to delay it so you can steal a little cream again."

Between them, Brenna watched the exchange like a tennis match, back and forth. Thorn scowled, clearly pissed. But Cameron's fingers were right there, dripping with her juice. They snagged Thorn's gaze, distracted him from his anger. He flipped his gaze up to Cameron, and a long, silent moment ensued. Brenna was dying to know what they were thinking. There was something in the air she didn't understand...

"Never mind," Cameron said. "I'll taste her for myself."

As he began to draw his fingers away, Thorn grabbed his wrist and tugged. In the next moment, he parted red lips and took Cam's drenched fingers in his mouth. Cameron closed his eyes, his body shuddering. Was he enjoying the fact Thorn was sucking his fingers? She would have sworn he was straight as an arrow, but...was he?

And Thorn groaned in her ear. She heard loud sucking sounds. And inside her, he grew even harder, his thrusts inside her even more aggressive.

Had he enjoyed her flavor...or the fact it came from Cameron's skin? What exactly was going on here?

Whatever it was, Brenna couldn't deny that watching them was exciting the hell out of her.

She moaned and grabbed handfuls of Cameron's hair. With it, she pulled his mouth to hers again, and he kissed her with a frenzy that hadn't been there before.

"Glove up," Thorn demanded of Cam, his voice scratchy. "Fucking hurry or this is going to end before you've started."

With a last sweet press of lips, Cameron backed away and shucked his jeans, watching as they hit the floor. *Oh, holy hell!* He was built, and then some. Thorn was no slouch, but Cameron was somewhere between amazing and porn star. Thick, with a bulbous, blue-tinged head and heavy veins running its length. Brenna stared, wondering if she could take all that.

"Shit, man," Thorn choked. "No wonder all the women at the station love you."

Cameron rolled his eyes then knelt to Brenna. "Have you ever taken a man anally?"

She shook her head.

Something resigned crossed Cam's face then he looked at Thorn. "It should be you then. Have you ever..."

"Had anal sex? Hell, yeah."

"With an anal virgin?"

"Um...no. You?"

He swallowed. "Once."

Brenna got the feeling it wasn't a good experience. And she understood why. Cameron's size was intimidating. She'd heard anal sex the first time could be painful. It didn't take Einstein to figure out that maybe it hadn't gone well.

"I still think it should be you," Cameron added. "I'll walk you through it." He directed the comment to both of them, and somehow knowing that cool, calm Cam was running the show made her feel better.

She loved Thorn's aggressive side, but not this first time.

"Yeah," Thorn agreed, withdrawing from her body with obvious reluctance. "Good call."

Nodding, Cam extended his hand to Brenna and helped her to her feet, her eyes never leaving his. Dark and reassuring but aflame with desire, he singed her with a glance. Her belly clenched.

He squeezed her hand. "It's going to be okay. I promise."

Why she should trust him so freely with her body, she didn't know. An instinct? He wouldn't hurt her. He wasn't just a detective, he was on the side of right and justice. She felt that about him. And Thorn...he was all badass on the outside, but she was beginning to suspect the inside consisted of a marshmallow core. He'd had a thousand opportunities to hurt her, take utter advantage of her. But he hadn't. He'd waited, trying to bring her along. Of course, all that, at least in part, was because they wanted information. But she sensed that underneath the badge and the bluster, they were honestly good guys.

Thorn rose to stand beside them. Cam caressed her cheek then lay on the bed. As he repositioned himself on his back, his dark, muscled thighs spread, the bed squeaked and the mattress rattled. The stalk of his erection lay thick and flat against his belly. Thorn tossed him a condom in a shiny foil wrapper. Cam caught it one handed. With quick efficiency, he put it on.

This was happening. Really happening. She swallowed.

Cameron held out his hand to her. "Come here and be with us."

She could back out now. *And then what?* a voice in her head asked. She had nothing to lose and a lot of pleasure to gain. At the very least, she could check this fantasy off her list.

Thorn crowded behind her, caressing her hip as he urged

her toward the bed. Flattening her palm against her fluttering belly, she climbed over Cameron, who took her hips in his hands and guided her down until her chest rested against his, their mouths a breath apart. His thick erection burrowed into the canal of her pussy, between her lips. He was right there, but not inside her. The sensation of him pulsing against her, brushing over her clit, left her aching to be filled.

Beside her, Brenna heard Thorn rustling in the nightstand drawers, but she didn't spare him a glance, not when Cameron's gaze drizzled warmth and desire all over her.

A moment later, she felt something cool and liquid against her back entrance. She jumped.

"Hey," Thorn soothed. "Nothing bad. Just lube to ease the way."

Oh, lube. Okay...

Then Thorn's fingers were there, where no man's had ever been, spreading the liquid around, pressing it deep inside her. The sensation was...new but not unwelcome. Pressure, an unexpected tingle, then a sudden dark wash of pleasure that had her gasping.

"That feel okay?" Thorn asked as he slowly pumped a finger into her ass.

Okay? Try shockingly good. "Yeah."

He added another finger. The sensations doubled and a bite of pain tangled with everything that enthralled her. She sighed.

"Your face..." Cameron whispered. "You look gorgeous with your cheeks flushed. The way you keep biting that pretty bottom lip of yours is driving me insane."

He clasped her face in his hands and pulled her in for a kiss. Rather than the gentle patience she'd always associated with Cam, this kiss had an edge. He was losing his cool. Frenzy and impatience spiced the flow of his lips over hers. She tasted it when he licked at the seam of her lips and urged her to open for him.

The two of them were undoing her. Completely. Pleasure bombarded her from all directions, familiar but totally new. She'd been on edge for nearly an hour, and something inside her felt ready to detonate. Frustration and yearning collided, then mingled with the inexplicable need to mingle with Thorn and Cam.

It all ramped up again when the gorgeous bounty hunter reached around with his free hand and made lazy circles around her nipples. Cam nudged his cock against her clit in the same moment. She gasped.

"Still good?" he murmured, his voice husky and low in her ear.

Everything was hitting her at once, the individual sensations combining to make her one trembling mass.

She ripped her mouth away from Cam's kiss and cried out, "Thorn!"

"Here, baby. Right here."

Then there was movement behind her. Cam nodded.

Brenna knew what that meant. And she both wanted and feared it.

"Don't tense," Cam advised. "We're going to do this all together."

The words were nothing less than a promise. She took a deep breath.

Cam nodded slightly. Behind her, Thorn grabbed her hip with one hand. Then she felt the blunt tip of his cock pressing against her back entrance.

"Slow," Cam advised the other man. "Real slow."

Thorn's hand on her hip tightened but she knew he'd heard.

"Brenna," Cam whispered, snagging her attention away from Thorn long enough to hear, "Push out and down on him."

Arousal and an edge of fear tripped through her at his

words, but Cameron would be straight up with her. He'd never want to see her in pain. She did as she was told.

Slick friction preceded Thorn's thick erection sliding a little deeper. He pushed gently, testing, but something inside her was resisting his invasion.

"Push down more." Thorn's voice sounded like sandpaper over gravel.

He was restraining himself. She felt it in the trembling of his hand at her hip. She didn't know how much restraint he had left—and she didn't want to test him. Brenna forced herself to push again.

Then she felt the broad tip of him smashed against a barrier inside her. And he began to ease in slowly...but unrelentingly.

The pressure swamped her, becoming a pain all its own. He wasn't going to fit. Seriously. Maybe she wasn't built for this. Maybe Thorn was too big. Maybe—

"I can't get past her sphincter."

Cameron quickly intervened. "Draw back and start slow thrusts as far in as you can."

"Listen, man..." he began.

"Do it." Brenna would never have believed Cameron could growl but that was pretty damn close. Then he turned his dark stare to her. In those depths, she saw scorching lust. He wanted inside her. Bad. But he was doing his best to regard her with concern and reassurance.

With long strokes of his palm, Cameron rubbed her back and planted long, slow kisses on her neck, her cheek, the corner of his mouth. She melted against him.

"Good girl," he breathed against her ear. "That's it."

Absently, she nodded. She hadn't realized how tense she'd been.

Behind her, Thorn drew back, then slid forward again to the barrier—and deeper another inch. He withdrew and started over, getting a little farther inside her. She could feel herself stretching to accommodate him. The pressure was unavoidable, the pain a sharp cut inside her.

"What if I don't like this?" she asked, trying not to grit her teeth and tense again.

"Then I'm doing something wrong." Thorn sounded strained.

"We'll think of something else. But give him a chance," Cam cajoled.

Sighing to release more pent-up tension, she nodded.

Cameron lengthened his strokes down her back, now reaching all the way down to her backside. He began to pet her, caressing his way over her curves.

"You have a gorgeous ass. Just touching it turns me on. But if I knew that Thorn was deep inside you here..." He shuddered. "Even the thought makes me shake with lust."

She wanted that, Brenna realized. She wanted Cameron to be out of his head with need for her. Thorn, too, for that matter. At least for now. Later, she'd worry about their opinions when she couldn't orgasm. But for this moment, she wanted to glory in their adulation.

Gliding his palms over the cheeks of her ass, Cameron grabbed them and held them open for Thorn, who grunted and pushed forward again. Brenna did her best to relax, despite the unfamiliar burn and pressure, and push down. The sensations weren't pleasant, yet...she couldn't say it was exactly uncomfortable anymore.

Suddenly, her body gave way. The head of Thorn's cock popped past the barrier and he pushed in and in and in, until, with a groan, he slid up to the hilt.

"Oh, fuck," Thorn groaned. "She's tight."

"You're in?"

"Yeah." The syllable was more grunt than spoken word.

"Excellent," Cam praised, then asked her. "How do you

feel?"

Full. A lot of pressure, but shockingly, the pain was gone. In fact, it was as if a hundred nerve endings were now awakening. Dormant once, she'd never known or thought about them until they suddenly leapt to life. And when Thorn withdrew back to the barrier and plunged in again, tingles of arousal leapt from nearly flat line to off the charts.

She cried out and clutched at Cameron's shoulder with wide-eyed amazement.

His warm chuckle slid over her like melted chocolate. "I think that's a good sign. Keep going, but gently."

"If I do much more of this, I'm going to come in about five seconds like a damn teenager. Shit. She's so hot and just...everywhere around me."

"You need me to take over?" Cam challenged.

"Hell, no. Back the fuck off," Thorn snarled as he jetted deep inside her again.

Then he draped his chest over her back and his hands were everywhere—gliding over her shoulders, skating down her arms, caressing her breasts, manipulating hard nipples.

"I know you feel me deep," he whispered in her ear. "I sure as hell feel you. You're like fireworks, one explosive surprise after another. Only a matter of time before you set me off."

"Watching the two of you is burning me up," Cam whispered against her lips, his gaze dipping to Thorn's fingers manipulating the hard nubs of her nipples.

Cameron reached down and draped his fingers over her mound, then slid his fingers through her drenched folds, over her sensitive clit. The moment he touched the tip, fire ripped up her belly, down her thighs. Brenna cried out. He did it again, and the tingles were heaping arousal on top of screaming sensation. It was overloading her, pouring heat and need over her and melting her like hot chocolate over ice cream.

Thorn compounded it all with another endless stroke deep in her ass. Then another. She arched her back, and he settled in another fraction of an inch. "Fuck!"

"That's next on my agenda." Cameron settled into a rhythm, petting her in the very spot that made her flare with need. "I want you good and wet when I take you."

Something inside her was tightening. Her insides began to pulse slowly. Blood was rushing to her sex.

"I'm there," she gasped. "Way there."

"I can tell," he said wryly. "But the goal here is to make you come."

"I'm close." The words came out in a whimper between pants. But her body was tense, fired—seconds from something amazing.

The hard breaths all around ramped her up even more. Thorn's exhalation settled against her neck, Cameron's in her ear. She heard her own against Cam's chest. The sounds of sex echoed deep in her body, brought along by the tang of sweat, and moans and desire.

"Damn it, I'm close too," Thorn barked, tense behind her. "Get inside her and fuck her already."

"I'm not rushing this." Cam muttered a curse then reached lower down her body before his touch disappeared.

Suddenly, Thorn cried out. "What the fuck! Get your goddamn hands off my balls."

Shocked, Brenna stared into Cam's face, where she found both lust and amusement. Wow, there had to be something more going on between Cam and Thorn. Was Cam making a move on Thorn?

"Get over it." Cam brought his hand up again and began to fondle her clit again. "Tugging on them kept you from coming, right?"

Thorn muttered something that sounded suspiciously like *son of a bitch*. "Yeah, but if you do it again, you're going to be minus a hand."

"If I hadn't done it, we were going to be minus a satisfied woman. We agreed to the purpose and the means. Stay on the bandwagon."

Again, Thorn muttered. Brenna distinctly heard *prick*.

So these two weren't in the habit of touching one another. The thought that they might, maybe someday, aroused her. She had no idea why. The thought of two guys touching each other had never entered her imagination before. But something about Cam's controlled gentleness and Thorn's wild passion colliding set her off.

Cameron took hold of her hips and slowed Thorn's increasingly rapid thrusts. The bounty hunter gritted his teeth so hard, she could swear she heard the bones of his jaw grinding.

But Brenna couldn't focus on that when Cameron fitted the blunt head of his cock against her entrance and started pushing.

He'd done his job well, making her wet to slick his way inside smoothly. So smooth. An anguished moan tore from her chest. The usual burn of being stretched melded with the added sensation of being smaller than usual, thanks to Thorn's erection in her ass.

"Holy mother…" Thorn trailed off in a gravel voice.

"It's amazing," Cameron agreed, strained, as he slid in deep, deep, deeper—then kept going.

With a groan, she bit into Cam's shoulder. God, he felt huge. The two of them together were overwhelming, incredible, surrounding her completely, front and back. Thorn's sweat-slicked chest and five o'clock shadow covered her back. Cam's hard pecs, lust-dark eyes and urgent hands, kept her right against his body.

Thorn withdrew, then pushed in as Cameron pulled back. Like counterparts of a piston, they fucked her in turn.

Never, ever, when they'd suggested this impromptu

ménage a trois had she imagined it would feel this…

Perfect.

Being sandwiched between them, Brenna felt surrounded, cocooned. And…safe. Cared for. Wanted like never before. Endlessly adored.

Inside, she felt herself clamping down on them as they rode her slowly, but thoroughly, wrenching one moan after another out of her.

"Brenna?" Cam sounded like he'd run a marathon. "You're getting tighter on me."

"Us," Thorn clarified. "And it's fucking killing me."

"You feel me?" Cam asked.

"Yes." Brenna's voice shook.

"I know *you* do. I'm making sure of that." To drive his point home, he pushed his way deep inside her in that moment, nudging her cervix with his tip.

Fresh tingles threatened to detonate everywhere. Dizziness tinged the edge of her vision. She could hardly catch a breath. Her skin felt damp, her limbs boneless. Her blood was on fire.

And she loved it.

"I meant you." Cameron shot Thorn a challenging glance. "Can you feel me?"

Chapter Six

🔊

Cameron withdrew then gritted his teeth as Thorn sank deep in her ass. "I sure as hell feel you."

"Yeah," Thorn croaked. "Hard to miss you. Jesus, this is insane. Hot!"

"Beyond hot."

Brenna couldn't agree more, but it was more than hot. Cameron's mouth crashed over hers, drawing her closer and closer to him in a way that was more than physical. Thorn reached around her hip and began to toy with her clit again.

"Ever shared before?" Cameron asked Thorn over Brenna's shoulder.

"No. Fuck!" he cried out. "I'm already addicted. I'm going to need more of this."

"Definitely." Cam's agreement was a sexy purr against her throat.

They wanted her. To stay with her. No, it wasn't permanent, but she already knew that nothing was. In this moment, in some odd way, she mattered to them. Her pleasure mattered to them. All the grunts, strokes, sweating and straining, the aching, trying to hold back, the reassuring, gentle caresses and sexy banter—that was all for her.

The sensations pinging all through her body began to migrate, to congeal, into a deep pulse of need between her legs. She'd never felt anything like it. Like she had to explode or die. She held her breath. Black spots danced at the edge of her vision. She felt herself clamping down on Cam and Thorn. They clutched at her, gripping, sliding deep, possessing her.

"You're right there, baby," Thorn growled as he swiped

another thick finger right across the tip of her clit. "Fuck, yeah. When you come, it's going to blow my mind."

"Fall," Cam coached. "We'll catch you."

Then, in a rush, all the blood in her body seemed to soar to her sex, heating, burning. The pressure built, the pleasure stacked up. God, it was huge, a tidal wave of ecstasy. She was going to implode from the force if it gave way.

Thorn rubbed at her clit again, his drenched fingers sliding around the sensitive nub, then right over the top again, just as Cam slid balls-deep again. The friction of his entrance, coupled with Thorn's exit…

Everything inside her went *kaboom!*

Brenna shook, jolted, spasmed with the force of the monster climax. As pleasure tore through her body and her sex throbbed, she screamed and clutched at Cameron. Orgasm turned her inside out, reformed her opinion about her body and sex. Shocked her. And still, they kept on. Cam's teeth in her shoulder, Thorn's shout in her ear, and their frenetic thrusts inside her, as if they had to wring every ounce of sensation out of her body or die, told her they, too, felt the effects of arousal overload.

Oh. My. God. This was what she'd been missing out on all her life? If she'd known, she would have sought these two out sooner. Because she knew that not just any two guys would do—they were special.

But now what? They didn't want a lifelong partnership or anything. Not that she did. They wanted information about Curtis, first and foremost.

Would they believe her, hate her—or both—once they knew the truth?

* * * * *

A few snatched hours of sleep and a shower later, Thorn sat at the kitchen table, watching the sun rise over the mountains and Brenna fry bacon wearing only a pair of lacy panties and an apron. She hummed absently.

After her orgasm, which seemed to double as an earthquake, she'd conked out and left him with two mutually exclusive desires—to pry information about Curtis out of her and fuck her again.

Her deep, even breathing told him neither was happening.

Instead, he'd taken in the sight of her curled up against him, then looked over her, to Cameron. So now they'd shared a woman. And the way Cameron was caressing her shoulder and looking mighty comfortable, the good detective clearly wasn't going to relinquish her. Well, tough shit. Neither was he, not after the way she'd rocked his world. Not after the way they'd rocked hers. Knowing they'd been the first to give her real pleasure had been an aphrodisiac all its own. Usually, the women he took to bed were going to get off—it was a given.

Brenna was…different—in a million ways. And he wasn't budging from her side until he figured out exactly why that mattered to him.

Finally, Cameron had opted for the shower first, giving him a few precious moments alone with Brenna. He hadn't spoken, hadn't touched her. Just basked in the weird gut instinct that told him he belonged next to her at that moment.

Which made no fucking sense.

Now, with the desert sun inching over the mountains to beam in the wide kitchen window, Brenna seemed to glow, especially when she glanced at him with a smile.

The domesticity of the scene went straight to his dick. Then again, so did everything else she did.

"You're frowning," she observed.

Normally he didn't give a shit what his lay the night before thought the morning after. Hell, he was never there to care. They were good for a fuck. If he saw them the next day, it usually wasn't his choice. And if they'd made such a statement, he would have found the most expedient way to tell them to get lost.

Again, Brenna was unique.

"Thinking," he offered, his voice rusty. "Got anything to drink?"

"Coffee, orange juice…" She opened the refrigerator. "Iced tea, a little bit of milk…"

He'd actually been fishing for vodka. If he was going to face actually giving a shit about someone, he wasn't sure he wanted to do it sober.

Damn, that apron she'd put on over the scrap of black panties was giving him a hell of a hard-on. He'd never seen a woman wear an apron before. Or had one cook for him. When she set a steaming plate of eggs, bacon and toast in front of him, his first reaction had been to get her flat on the table and nail her. He gripped the arm of the chair to resist the urge, since he and Cam had already given her a workout.

"Something wrong?"

"No. I just…" He glanced between the plate and her expectant face framed by her haphazardly pinned up honey-brown hair. Finally, he cleared his throat. "Thank you."

"You're welcome." She set another plate down beside him. "Tell Cam this is his when he gets off the phone."

Absently, he nodded and reached for a fork to dig in when he realized she was leaving the room. He grabbed her wrist instead. "Where you going, baby?"

"I don't usually eat breakfast." She wrinkled her lightly freckled nose. "I'm going to get the newspaper so I can read it while you eat."

Reluctantly, he dropped her hand. She disappeared around the corner, and he dug into the food. She emerged a few moments later with her hair hanging loose, wearing sweatpants and a t-shirt, no bra. With a smile, she walked past him, and Thorn heard the front door shut. He sighed. His appetite wasn't really for breakfast, but there was no sense in letting good food go to waste.

He bit into a slice of crispy bacon and just about fell in love. Done but not burnt. The woman could cook—a valuable ability to a man who'd never known home cooking and couldn't cook worth a damn for himself.

Cameron strolled in from the backyard a moment later, tucking his phone onto his belt. "Nothing new. No one has seen Lawton. They've widened the APB. He's been gone long enough to put some serious mileage between himself and Tucson by now."

"Agreed." Thorn nodded to the plate. "I'm supposed to tell you that's your breakfast."

"I know better than to think you cooked."

Thorn just snorted and rolled his eyes.

"Brenna?"

"Getting the paper."

"What did you think of last night?" Cam sat and shoveled a bite of egg in his mouth.

Damn, just like it was casual conversation. *How's the weather? Good. How was the fuck?*

Sneaky bastard.

"It was fine."

Cam raised a dark brow. "Just fine?"

"Yep."

"What about it wasn't better than fine?"

Thorn dropped his fork to his plate with a clatter. "Look, Oprah, I'm not talking about my 'feelings'. We shared a woman. It was good. End of story."

In response, Cam just smiled. Before he even spoke, Thorn just knew that whatever came out of the detective's mouth was going to piss him off.

"I don't think that's the end of the story. I think you're itching to do it again."

He was, and the fact Cameron was right... It just added to

his increasingly weird mood. First, Brenna had to cook a perfect breakfast and remind him of all he'd never had. Then the good detective had to add to his shit by rubbing his nose in the fact Thorn had liked sharing a woman.

But weird mood or not, the vision of Cameron's dark hands gliding across Brenna's fragile, pale skin while Thorn sank into the hot glove of her ass made him sweat. Remembering the feel of Cam on the other side of that thin membrane, deep in her pussy, rubbing his dick with every stroke just about killed him.

Fuck. This wasn't good.

"I don't do the same woman twice if it can be avoided."

Cam finished off his bacon then shrugged. "Okay. We still have to tail her until we get some information about Curtis. But if you're not interested in dipping from the well twice…I have no such qualms. I guess you can watch."

Hell. "You're a prick."

Wiping his mouth, Cam tried to hide his smile with his napkin. He did a lousy job. Laughter danced in his dark eyes.

Thorn restrained the urge to punch him—barely. "What the hell is the matter with you, man? Why are you pushing for more?"

His smile dissolved. "Together, you and I gave Brenna something she's never had and couldn't even give herself. That was amazing for me. She gets to me, and I want to satisfy her even more."

"I thought for sure it would bug the shit out of you that you couldn't make her come all by yourself."

"When we were both inside her, I felt as…close to her as I would if we were alone. Having you there didn't detract from the experience. I felt a bond, and I want more of that."

Thorn swallowed. Yeah, he'd felt that same closeness and bond—and not just with Brenna. God, had he really just admitted that? This whole fantasy was turning nightmare, and it scared the shit out of him.

The feelings reminded him of the time he'd wanted to keep a stray kitten he'd found just before his eleventh birthday. New, wonderful. The sense of caring and connection was something he'd never had. Unfortunately, it was short-lived, since his dad had drowned the kitten in the toilet. Thorn knew that if his father were here now, dear old Dad would find some equally loathsome way to squash these burgeoning feelings too. And probably with good reason. What the hell kind of pansy ass shared a woman with another guy and liked it? Much less admitted that sharing her made him feel closer, not just to her, but the other guy?

Thorn wasn't gay, but being with Brenna had felt a bit like sharing sex with not just her, but Cam too. The shit part was, he'd really gotten into it.

This whole scene was too damn unsettling. Hard dick or not, he was folding.

"Knock yourself out," Thorn said. "I'm done."

"So you're just going to watch and pretend that she isn't important to you?"

"Pretty much." And it was going to hurt like hell. Which bugged him even more.

"Why? Why not follow your instincts, your feelings—"

"Man, I'm not wired like you. I just don't have feelings. I'm a heartless bastard with a drive-through sex life, remember? You said it yourself. Back the fuck off."

Cam paused for the longest minute. Finally, he stood, grabbed his plate, and headed for the sink, something, no doubt, sage and clever perched on his tongue.

The squealing of tires, followed by gun fire and Brenna's scream cut through everything. Thorn leapt up from his chair and set out at a flat run.

Chapter Seven

ॐ

Thorn charged out the front door, .38 in hand, looking both poised and pissed as hell. Didn't matter that he was without both shirt and shoes, his tangled hair hanging in pale strands to his shoulders. In leather pants and nothing else, he looked like a Viking warrior of old, big and bad and someone no one sane fucked with. That he was charging out half dressed... Didn't that speak volumes about what he wasn't willing to say out loud?

Of course, Cam was right behind him, weapon drawn, heart beating in a vicious pound. What had spooked Brenna? Was someone shooting at her, at *their* woman?

No time now to examine why he felt that way. Cam knew there'd be time later, after they put a stop to whatever threatened her, to think about the fact that, while this had been the first time he and Thorn had shared her, it wouldn't be the last.

Running, his booted feet pounded concrete until he cleared the front courtyard. Tall strands of yucca plants blocked the slice of street visible from this angle.

Finally, he rounded the corner to the street, a half step behind Thorn.

"Fuck!" the bounty hunter growled.

Then he feinted left, planted and aimed his gun.

Cameron didn't even wait to see the threat before he got in position. As he was steadying his weapon, he finally got a glimpse of the scene—and could barely contain his rage.

A tricked-out sports car had been slung haphazardly in the cottage's driveway. A thug in a white tank top that hung loosely from his doubtless drug-addicted frame chased Brenna in a circle around the vehicle. As she neared the driver's side window, another asshole rolled down the window and pointed a gun right at her chest. The second she saw it, she gasped and slapped a trembling hand over her mouth.

"Oh God. No! I'll give you money…"

"No more warnings. Shut up, bitch, and get in the car," growled the voice from the auto's interior.

No one was taking Brenna anywhere.

Usually one to keep the peace, Cam welcomed the sudden feeling of wanting to cram their balls down their throats as he read them their rights.

The car door opened, and a figure emerged, his gun still trained on her. He was a short man, bald and unfamiliar. But with the look of leather and the 70s porn-star moustache, he had to be one of Julio Marco's lackeys.

Brenna backed away with her hands up, and the goon with the dirty wife-beater shirt grabbed her shoulders roughly. Beside Cam, Thorn tensed.

"Don't fire," he hissed at the bounty hunter.

"Bullshit! I won't let them take—"

"I'll do it. Sneak around to the side yard and back me up."

After hesitating, Thorn took off to get in place. Within moments, the bounty hunter crouched behind a huge bird of paradise plant some ten yards away and nodded.

Taking a deep breath, Cam focused on the criminals, and did his best to block Brenna's terrified cries of "no, please" out of his head as she dug in her heels while they dragged her closer to the open car door. If he squeezed this shot off right, he'd have time to comfort her later.

Briefly, he thought of having Thorn call for backup. No time, first of all. Second, admitting that he'd spent the night with someone who was potentially aiding and abetting an alleged felon wasn't exactly high on the ethical charts. Besides, they had surprise on their side.

"Freeze. Police!" he shouted.

As he hoped, the two criminals jolted, momentarily taking their eyes off Brenna as they scanned the area, searching for the source of the warning. Brenna took advantage of their distraction and jabbed her elbow into the concave abdomen of the meth head, who grunted and clutched his belly, and released her.

She darted back toward the house.

Not about to let her go, Baldy raised his gun and pointed it at her back.

Cam fired off a warning shot, barely missing the guy with the gun—on purpose. The bullet pinged off his souped-up red pimpmobile. He would have simply shot the asshole, but he wasn't worth the paperwork—at least so far. If he threatened Brenna again, Cam vowed he'd use the greasy bastard's forehead for target practice.

Out of nowhere, Thorn appeared and snagged Brenna around the waist, soothing her with a whisper as he dragged her safely into hiding.

Breathing easier now, Cameron met the threat of the two thugs head on.

"Backup is on the way. Stay where you are," he reached for his cuffs and lied through his teeth, knowing there was no way in hell they'd comply.

Julio Marco was aggressive and liked to win. But if getting caught was likely, that was to be avoided at all costs. And if his hired guns were taken into police custody, Marco would deny all knowledge of them. Their lives would be worth next to nothing after that.

Judging by the way they hauled ass into the car, slammed doors and squealed tires away from Curtis' cottage, they knew it too.

But he didn't have time for sighs of relief.

Jogging across the cactus and gravel yard, he pushed past the metal gate and found Thorn and Brenna safe and in one piece—almost literally.

With his back to the concrete fence that separated the cottage's pool area from scrub and desert, Thorn had wrapped muscled arms around Brenna's huddled form. She burrowed into the safety of his bare chest. With one hand on his gun and the other in her hair, he whispered and soothed her, pressing hot, hard kisses to her lips.

If the situation hadn't been so damn dire, he would have smiled.

As soon as Thorn saw Cam, he tensed. "They gone?"

"Yes."

Thorn tucked his gun into the waistband at the small of his back then tightened his arms around Brenna, who was stiff and trembling against him. "It's okay, baby. You're safe."

"For how long?"

Good question. The fact that Julio Marco's goons were here and threatening Brenna with violence told him two things—one, Marco didn't have the faintest clue where Curtis had slipped away to, and two, the human smuggler knew that Brenna was important enough to Curtis to want to abduct her and use her as leverage.

The time for Mr. Nice Guy had come to an end.

"Pack a bag," Cameron barked. "Quick. We need to be out of here in five minutes."

"What... Why?"

"They'll be back with reinforcements and enough fire power to blow up the side of this mountain."

"Oh." She bit her lip. "Can't we call the police?"

"Sure, but they'll take you in to question you about Curtis' disappearance. And you're insane if you think Julio Marco can't get to you there. We'd be barred from protecting you. I'm not comfortable with that."

"I like my odds better with you. Where are we going?"

Cameron paused. "My place. You're going to tell us about your relationship with Curtis and what you know of his whereabouts."

He turned and made his way to the back door, jimmying the lock with a credit card and a few seconds' patience.

"How did you do that?" Thorn demanded.

"I wasn't always a cop," he said over his shoulder with a smile.

* * * * *

In a handful of minutes, Brenna had dressed and tossed her belongings back into her suitcase. That wasn't hard, considering the fact she'd barely unpacked when she arrived in Arizona. She heard clattering in the kitchen and assumed Cameron was doing his best to clean up after breakfast. Thorn was watching her with an unblinking stare, his laser gaze following her around the room as she grabbed the last of her belongings.

The intensity of that gaze dredged up memories that weren't conducive to efficient packing. She was basically fleeing for her life. Why was her gaze clinging to Thorn? Why the hell was she wet?

"Stop staring," she snapped. "You're making me nervous."

He rolled his bare shoulders then bent to pick up the vest he'd discarded last night, followed by his boots. "It's either stare at you or fuck you. We don't have time for the latter."

True. And she should be relieved. He and Cam had been overwhelming last night, and she was still shocked by what she'd done, and the fact that, for them, she had had an almighty orgasm so powerful, it had nearly blown her head off. But she wasn't relieved that the situation now demanded prudence. She was annoyed. And scared.

Exiting the bathroom with the last of her toiletries, she stuffed them into a bag. As soon as she emerged, Thorn propelled her back, holding out a wide palm to slam the door behind her before he shoved her against it. Brenna dropped her bag with a gasp as he fitted his body against hers, his mouth hovering right over her own. She couldn't mistake the erection digging into the apex of her thighs.

"But we're going to make time later. A whole lot of time."

His voice was a rumble that vibrated through her, exciting every nerve ending inside her that had lain dormant for...well, her whole life.

She'd always felt the sting of abandonment just beneath her skin. Like people could see her version of the scarlet letter, a big, black A on her forehead that shouted the fact she'd never been wanted, that everyone would always leave her. And should, as if she somehow deserved it.

It didn't feel like Thorn was going anywhere anytime soon.

"We should go," she whispered breathlessly.

"That's the only thing keeping clothing on your body now, baby."

Aggressive. But she'd known Thorn was from the moment he'd awakened her after tying her to Curtis' bed. She shivered.

"Now," said Cam from the doorway of the bedroom, where he took in the scene with watchful eyes, "We need to get you in the truck. And you need to tell us everything you know about Curtis."

It was time.

And then...then she'd see how long they stayed.

*   *   *   *   *

Three minutes later, they were piled into the bench seat of Cam's pick up, Brenna in the middle. Thorn's cycle lay in the truck's bed. Normally, he'd never surrender his bike for a ride with a cop in sleek black truck.

When the hell had staying beside Brenna and hearing her story become more important?

If he wanted his fifty thousand, he needed to hear whatever she knew about Curtis and his whereabouts, but Thorn feared his refusal to unglue himself from her side was more than that. And although he was hard as concrete for her, it wasn't just sex. But defining it… Nope, he wasn't going there.

"How do you know Curtis?" Cameron laid a gentle hand on her knee and squeezed as they drove away from Lawton's cottage. "We need to know what we're up against."

She hesitated, pausing to glance at him then Cam. She swallowed. "He's my father."

Thorn's jaw dropped. He couldn't have been more surprised if she'd said she was a three-breasted alien from Jupiter.

Her gaze met his again then skittered away. She focused on her wringing hands in her lap. "I see you're shocked."

"I shouldn't be, I suppose," Cam said. "I knew you weren't his mistress."

"I never believed he'd let you stay at his place if you were just a friend of a friend," Thorn added.

But daughter? *Man…*

"We aren't close." Brenna licked her lips. "In fact, I hadn't seen him since my high-school graduation. Before that…he left me with my aunt when I was a baby."

What the fuck? For all that his old man had been a lousy parent, he'd never dumped him on someone else's doorstep. Nope, good old Ronald had kept him around for every lousy, squalor- and hunger-filled day, cementing in his head the fact that drugs were thicker than blood.

"He gave me away shortly after my mother died. He let

my aunt and her husband adopt me, signed away all parental rights." Her face flushed, and she frowned, fighting tears. "As an adult, I knew his abandonment had affected my ability to have a relationship. Until January, I was engaged. Great guy. But my...coldness made him feel like a failure, and he couldn't accept that the failing was mine. So..."

"So you parted ways," Cam finished.

She nodded.

"You couldn't come because piece-of-shit Curtis ditched his responsibility." Thorn told it like it was, and the anger over that fact made him want to pound the dirtbag's face.

"Pretty much, yes."

"And then your fiancé couldn't hack it?"

"Yes."

"Asshole," Thorn muttered.

Cameron squeezed her knee again, then glided his hand up her thigh, up, up... Thorn thought of all the things that hand might do to Brenna and started to sweat.

"Something about being with us changed that." Cam didn't ask, just stated.

"With both of you near me, surrounding me, inside me..." She flushed. "I felt protected. The way you enveloped me, it was like I would never be alone again. You two filled me so full, it felt right." She shrugged. "It was somehow easy to believe that I was worthy of your desire and that you'd just...I don't know. Like you'd always be there for me. But I don't expect anything," she was quick to assure. "I know it was just the one night."

For some reason, her words pissed Thorn off. Despite what he'd told Cam, *he'd* say when they were done, damn it.

Which made no sense. He hadn't planned to stick around, and was still torn between keeping his distance and indulging the hunger for her sizzling in his veins and licking at his balls. Now... Thorn would walk away when the time came, he always did. But knowing he'd been instrumental in helping her accomplish something that had always eluded her, that he'd helped her to feel something she'd needed so badly... Well, it was heady. And he wasn't sure how could just turn his back.

Why the fuck did she matter?

And why the hell did seeing Cam's hand absently caressing her make him hard?

Thorn tore his gaze away from the two of them and glanced out the windshield, glancing at the side mirrors. The morning rush hour was beginning to pick up, so it was impossible to determine if they were being trailed by Marco's heavies.

"How far away?" he asked. "We have to get out of sight quickly."

Cam sent him a sharp nod, checking the side mirrors himself. "I don't see that we're being followed but it's hard to tell. Too many cars... My place is close, the address secret, but if you have a better idea..."

"No. Fuck... Every criminal in creation knows how to find me. Your place works. We just need to get into hiding. Being out in the open is making me itchy."

Brenna placed a calming touch on his arm. "Thank you."

For what? He hadn't done nearly enough to keep her safe, or she wouldn't have been in any danger this morning. That little furrow between her brows said that she was...concerned about him. Worried, even. Amazing. She'd nearly been abducted this morning and *she* was calming *him*?

Sweet southern sugar with a hint of sass, that was Brenna. She melted like fine chocolate between him and Cam. She soothed like silk when she thought they were worried. This was a new female for him. She wasn't here for the party or for the sex, the ride with a bad boy or a good time. Why was she here, beyond wanting to feel like a whole woman? Why trust them?

"You look so damn calm, baby," he commented.

She sent him a soft smile. "You two are with me."

As if that said it all. Already, after just a few hours, she trusted them. Wow. He'd never been anyone's savior and would have bristled at the suggestion in the past. He had his own shit to deal with. But Brenna... She needed him for more than his dick or his ability to fuck her multiple times a night.

Did he have more to give? And what about Cam?

Thorn leaned around Brenna to find the detective calmly driving. A right turn off the main drag, a left turn onto a residential street. A direct glance from those all-seeing dark eyes right into his.

Cam was going to fight—not him for the right to be with Brenna, but to keep the three of them together. What the hell? A *ménage* was fun every so often but for more than a night? No, he had to be reading Cam's expression wrong. Right?

With a glance out the mirrors and the back window as they wound through Cam's neighborhood completely alone, it was clear that they'd shaken Marco's thugs—for now.

Though Thorn knew better than to imagine that would last, that did leave them plenty of time to explore exactly what would happen next between him and Cam and Brenna.

* * * * *

Tread carefully. Cam repeated the words to himself more than once.

After pulling into his garage, he helped Brenna from his SUV and into the deserted confines of his house. She was skittish. Thorn followed them, downright jumpy.

The unexpected visit from Marco's goons had shaken the big bounty hunter up way more than expected, and that gave Cam hope. If Thorn didn't give a rat's ass about Brenna, he would have celebrated the fact he'd had a fight on his hands. The fact his instinct had been to shield Brenna, then get out of the action and soothe her? Very interesting…

Cam himself wasn't sure exactly why he was pursuing this…thing with Thorn and Brenna so hard. The sex had been off-the-charts amazing. He'd been elated to help Brenna with her orgasm problem. Everything about her turned him on, and he even liked her on the inside. The fact she was Curtis Lawton's daughter threw a kink in the mess, but the issue wasn't insurmountable.

The addition of Thorn was an interesting dynamic. They weren't good friends. What shocked Cam over and over was how natural the three of them had felt together. How aroused he'd been just by watching Thorn tunnel into Brenna's tight body.

Sometimes Cam calculated his every move, calmly considering what to do next, even taking days or weeks to decide. This wasn't one of those times. Every instinct now screamed at him to do whatever necessary to keep the three of them together.

As Cam entered the house, he drew his weapon and looked around, throwing closets open and checking around dark corners. They were alone. Good. Now they could deal with the business at hand.

"Looks like we're all clear," he told them.

Thorn visibly relaxed, though his arm was still wound around Brenna's waist. Cam's gaze lingered on the way she clung to Thorn's mostly bare torso. The poor woman had been through an avalanche of crap lately, and he knew better than to think it was over.

"Good. You going to call this one in to the station?" Thorn asked.

"I'll run the plate on the car. Fifty bucks says it was reported stolen recently and that we'll find it ditched a few miles from Curtis' little cottage."

Swearing under his breath, the bounty hunter nodded. "You're right. What now?"

"Come in." He turned and led them deeper into the house. "Anyone hungry? Thirsty?"

After both murmured "no", he guided them into the living room. Cam purposely avoided the room's lone oversized chair and sat at one end of the sofa. Thorn plopped down on the other end, putting Brenna between them—as it should be. He set his gun down on the table within easy reach. Thorn did the same.

"What did those two jerks want with me?" Brenna asked, looking between him and Thorn.

"Who else knows you're Lawton's daughter?" Thorn asked.

Brenna scoffed. "Doubtful anyone does. It's not like we attended a lot of happy father-daughter events together. Even if this Julio Marco you've talked about does know, he should also know that I mean nothing to Curtis. And why would they want leverage over him?"

"I'm guessing," Thorn started, "that if Marco is looking for leverage against Lawton that he knows his partner in crime has turned on him and that Marco has no idea where he is."

"Agreed." Cam turned to Brenna. He hated to heap more on her after she'd had a torrid *ménage a trois* and nearly been abducted in the last twelve hours. But her life might depend on it. "You have absolutely no idea where your father is? My…our job is to ensure he makes it to the trial whole and alive so he can testify and put this scumbag away. He's already been offered and accepted immunity in exchange. I heard a whisper that the Feds agreed to enter him into the Witness Protection Program. Marco is big-time scum, and both the state and Feds want him behind bars. Your father's testimony could lock Marco away for good, and everyone knows it."

Brenna shook her head and cuddled up against his side. "Honestly, I have a cell phone number. He hardly ever answers it. I can try. I'll just need to unpack my purse and phone."

Cam opened his mouth to reply but stopped short when he saw Thorn's hand snake out to curl around Brenna's thigh.

"In a little bit, baby. You've had enough shit for the moment."

"Marco is going to come after me again, isn't he?"

"He'll have to find you first." Thorn sounded like a demon with a case of bad temper. "And get through me."

"Us," Cam corrected.

"I can't stay here forever. I'm invading your home…" She looked at Cam with apology.

"Hey…" He caressed her cheek. "This isn't your fault. It's Lawton's and Marco's. I'm sorry you're caught in the middle. And it's not forever." At least not yet. "The trial starts Monday. If your father shows up and testifies, they might kill him for spite but I think they'll leave you alone."

"So I'm imposing on you until then?"

"It's no imposition." He kissed her softly. "Trust me."

"I won't get in the way, I promise. I know you're busy with work and…whatever. You won't even know I'm here."

"I have vacation time coming. I'll call in for a few days. I plan on being by your side every day and night until that trial."

"What the fuck?" Thorn exploded, turning to Brenna. "You think I'm going to just fucking walk off when Marco is sending his hired guns to take you?"

She shrugged as she looked between the two of them. "Considering I didn't know either of you twenty-four hours ago, it would be wrong of me to expect you—"

"Caring isn't always about how long you've known someone." Unable to resist, Cam brushed a kiss over her lips. "I won't leave you to be a victim, either. It's not in me as a cop or a man."

With a nod, Brenna accepted that. "What about you?" she

said to Thorn. "I know you must have other bounties. I doubt you signed up to baby-sit me."

"You didn't sign up to handle with Curtis' shit but here you are. I'll deal. My brother can take some of the other bounties on my list. Between the three of us, we should be able to track your dad down and keep you safe."

Her eyes watered as she looked between the two of them. She wore her heart there, right in those pretty hazel eyes. And it was getting under Thorn's skin, based on the way his hand tightened on her thigh and he dragged her against him and crushed her mouth under his for a long, demanding kiss.

Cameron smiled. Things were about to get mighty interesting…

Chapter Eight

∞

Thorn was drowning. Like Pavlov's dog, he'd already equated the flavor of Brenna's kiss with mind-bending pleasure. So with the first caress of his tongue against hers, his cock rose stiff and tight and impatient.

But it wasn't just Brenna.

Even with his eyes closed, Thorn could feel Cam's dark gaze zeroed in on them. He didn't blink when Thorn deepened the kiss, when he slid a hand up her thigh, when he tugged the tank top over her head and confirmed that underneath, she wore absolutely nothing.

As he fell into Brenna's sweet taste, he couldn't hold back his moan. It wasn't enough, not even close. He wanted her closer, wanted more than her mouth under his. Thorn wasn't a man used to denying what he wanted. If Cam wanted to watch—fine. His cock tightened painfully at the thought of the detective joining in again.

Thorn couldn't comprehend his reaction. He was a selfish bastard who liked everything the way *he* liked it. Usually he wanted a woman all to himself because he was going to use her hard and well until neither of them could take any more. Sex wasn't a team sport, damn it. He preferred to control the game.

But last night... Having Cam on the team added an element of arousing unpredictability.

As he nibbled at Brenna's lips, he opened his eyes to find Cam's gaze following every move. Thorn's cock thickened again, pressing against the back of his zipper. The burn of desire seared deep and drove him out of his mind. He closed his eyes and sank back into the kiss.

Fuck whatever he *usually* liked, he was just going to flow with it. Besides, the bigger issue here was Brenna. She was shaken up. Totally understandable. As any guy who'd ever been in a fight could tell you, the best way to come off the adrenaline high was a good fuck. That's where he came in.

Clasping his arms around her, Thorn planned to lift her onto his lap, her chest to his, her firm little thighs wrapped around his hips. *Oh, yeah.* But when he tried, she wouldn't budge.

Thorn opened his eyes, not breaking the kiss, and discovered another pair of arms around her, another man holding her on his lap. Cam had clearly worked his way under Brenna, who sat on his lap, her back to his chest... And Cam's hands all over her body.

"That kiss good?" Cam murmured, looking right at him.

Thorn almost couldn't answer. The sight of the other man's bronzed, veined hand between her suddenly bare legs spiked his desire. When had Cam taken off her sweatpants?

Didn't matter. Brenna opened her thighs wider, and Thorn's whole body tightened. *Shit, this was getting hot fast.* Hot became explosive when he caught the unimpeded view of Cam's thick fingers tunnel inside Brenna's pussy then glide back out. He could see exactly how wet she was. The evidence made Cam's fingers glisten—and his own need to fuck her flipped off the charts.

His mouth hovering over Brenna's—his stare never leaving Cam's busy hand—he muttered. "Sweet. Man, how does she feel?"

"Tight and dripping. Ready to eat."

As soon as Cam said the words, Thorn's imagination filled him with a visual of the detective's dark head between Brenna's pale thighs. Even thinking about it spiked his need into the stratosphere.

"Do it," he baited. "Fucking do it and let me watch."

Brenna whimpered, and Thorn dropped a palm to

Brenna's exposed breasts, cradling one, thumbing its hard nipple. Cam watched with burning eyes, his fingers busy between her legs. Her pale skin was flushed, her head tossed back on Cam's shoulder, and with legs spread, it was a pose of utter surrender.

Shit, the burn incited by that view was about to eat Thorn alive.

"Do it," Thorn prompted again. "I want to see you make her come."

"Can I taste you, Brenna?" Cam whispered against her neck then dragged his lips across the sensitive joining between her neck and shoulder.

She shivered, shuddered then nodded. "Please…"

Thorn expected Cam to lay her flat on her back on the sofa and hunker down between her legs. He didn't. Instead, he ripped off his shirt then turned Brenna to face him so she straddled his lap.

"Kiss me," he demanded.

Brenna did, feathering her mouth over Cam's, a brush, a lingering swipe, then a deep sharing of tongues while the detective's hands roamed her back, her ass. And Thorn, hovering right beside them, was caught in the ultimate peep show, aroused out of his mind and loving it completely. What a wild trip.

Suddenly, Cam eased out of the kiss and caressed her. "Very nice. Would you be a sweet girl and let me see you kiss Thorn again?"

His gaze zipped over to the detective's. *He's getting off on this too. Holy shit!*

Her lashes fluttered shut against rosy cheeks, but a long moment later she nodded. Then she turned to him with hazel eyes dazed yet rich with sultry thoughts. He wanted to pounce on her, fuck her now. He wanted to see what would happen next just as bad. Decisions, decisions…

Thorn thrust his fingers into her honey brown hair and

used the long strands to guide her mouth under his. He slanted his mouth over hers, struck fast and deep and hard until she writhed against him and moaned. God, he could *smell* how wet she was, and it was going right to his cock.

When they broke apart, Thorn looked down to find Cam's white teeth nipping at Brenna's pebbled nipples. One after the other, then a soft suck, a brush of his tongue.

"Do that to her pussy," he demanded again.

With seeming reluctance, Cam lifted his mouth away from her breasts and slithered down on the leather sofa, until the back cushion propped up just his neck. Then he guided her to stand on her knees.

And suddenly, her pussy was right over his mouth. *Hot damn…*

Cam lifted his head and began devouring Brenna. She tossed her head back, gripping the back of the sofa. The curly ends of her hair teased the top of her ass, and Thorn wasn't sure he'd ever seen anything hotter. A flush crept across her whole body, and she began to pant, drawing in huge drafts of air.

"Oh my God…" Her voice trembled. She clutched at the sofa even tighter.

Thorn watched Cam's head move and bob between her legs and Brenna respond with utter abandon—and he nearly lost it. The time for being a spectator was gone. Now he wanted participate.

"Fuck, I need to taste her."

Cam turned his head to nip at her thigh. "She's about to come."

"I want my tongue on her when she does."

With a shake of his head, Cam refused. "Wouldn't you rather have her come around your cock?"

Was he suggesting…?

"You want me to fuck her pussy with your mouth on it?"

"Just a suggestion, man. If you want to be part of the experience, it was just a thought. Otherwise, I have no problem lapping it all up for myself."

As if to prove his point, Cam opened his mouth and sucked her clit inside. Brenna shrieked and grabbed the sofa cushion even harder.

"Cam…" she managed to eke out between panting breaths that lifted her breasts.

She was close again, and he was feeling uncomfortably close just watching them. He *wanted* to be in on the action. Fuck it. If Cam wasn't weirded out by having a man's dick near his mouth, Thorn refused to be weirded out by the fact another man had his mouth near his dick.

Like everything about this experience, he just needed to flow with it. *What the hell…*

Shucking his shirt and toeing off his shoes, Thorn dug into his wallet. Thankfully, another condom waiting just for the moment. He tore off his jeans and donned the rubber sheath in a handful of seconds.

He'd better hurry. Brenna's shrieks were becoming wails and pleas to a higher being.

"Hold her off. I'm almost there."

"No!" she protested. "No, I need…"

"We'll make sure you get it," Thorn vowed. "Just ease off a bit, man, until I get in."

Thorn didn't wait for confirmation. He stood behind Brenna, smoothed a flat palm across her back and gently pushed her down until her head rested on the back of the sofa.

He now had the perfect angle to slide into her pussy. And he didn't waste any time.

Gripping her hips, he slid inside Brenna, deep — all in a single glide. She was like hot silk, melting his spine and resistance all at once. How the hell was he supposed to hold out when he was already jacked up and she was all around his dick, shooting pleasure all through his body?

He reared back, plunged in again. And sucked in a shocked breath. *Damn!* So he repeated the process again. And again. Those old clichés about seeing stars and shit? Apparently that was true.

Then Cam started eating her pussy again, this time like a rabid animal. Every time the detective sucked on her clit and pulled it in his mouth, the walls of Brenna's sex pulsed, tightening until pushing into her was a workout in itself.

Sweat slicked his back. She was so damn tight, and the friction was overwhelming. She was going to short-circuit him in seconds. And still she kept clamping down on his cock the more Cam aroused her. Would he survive her actually coming?

Like a madman, he began pounding into her, pushing against the constriction of her pussy with long, ferocious strokes. Absently, he noticed that his balls were hitting something but with a brain so focused on the woman beneath him, it took a minute to realize that something was Cam's chin.

Oddly, the thought didn't repulse him. Not exactly. An odd shiver of tension wound its way up his spine. For a minute, he lost his rhythm, and Brenna clamped down again, this time so tight, she pushed him out.

She cried out in protest. Thorn flatly cursed and tried to reach between them, find his dick and push it back inside her. His hands shook too badly.

A moment later, he felt another hand grab his dick. Hot, large, knowledgeable as it stroked with just the right pressure in just the right place. Cam. *Holy shit!*

"What the hell are you doing?" he barked and tried to back away.

Cam had a tight hold on his cock, pumped him with his fist once or twice. It was like pouring electric juice in his veins. His system sizzled, damn near fried. Shock. Had to be shock.

Why did it feel so fucking much like pleasure?

Thorn gritted his teeth and resisted the urge to toss back his head with the overwhelming sensations. He struggled and tensed but Cameron tugged again, swiping a thumb over the sensitive crest once, twice.

With a curse ringing in his head, Thorn lost the battle, stared at the ceiling and hissed in a sharp breath through his teeth.

"What are you doing to me?"

Before Cam answered, he guided Thorn back to Brenna's waiting pussy. She was just as tight, and now even more aroused so that he felt every bit of her all around him. The memory of that solid hand touching him in all the right places pushed him so close to orgasm.

"She was going to cross the finish line before you," Cam explained. "So I helped you along."

And how…

Thorn was as straight as a guy could be, but…wow. Cam's touch had felt damn good — way too good for his peace of mind.

And then he wasn't thinking of anything as the detective's mouth covered Brenna's clit again. He sucked, she screamed, Thorn pushed in frantically against her pulsing walls — then the explosion came.

Huge. The thing was of mythical proportions. The feats of the Greek gods weren't nearly as amazing as this. The orgasm shot down his spine, burned and churned between his legs…then burst all the sensation through his body like a supernova spewing matter through the universe.

Oh. Holy. Fuck.

Long moments later, spent, he sagged over the damp skin of Brenna's back.

"Are you okay?" She looked over her shoulder at him.

He kissed her shoulder. Damn amazing woman. She'd just been tag teamed by two horny guys — twice in the last eight hours—and she worried about him. She'd cooked for him too. That slight Texas drawl was sweet, the equivalent of sugar for his dick.

"Fine, baby. You?"

She just hummed and let her body go even more limp.

And then there was Cam. Their...contact had not been strictly heterosexual. Hell, Thorn would make pulp of the asshole's face who suggested otherwise. But he'd be lying if he said he hadn't been affected by Cam's hands on his balls last night or stroking his dick just minutes ago. Even the thought, and interest stirred down south.

"As much fun as this party has been, I'm going to need a little relief," the detective said through gritted teeth.

Yeah, if he hadn't already come, he'd be a raving lunatic by now.

Thorn withdrew from Brenna's sweet body and sat on the couch, removing the condom. He tugged Brenna down on his lap, and she curled up against him, her head on his shoulder.

"Can you suck him, baby?" Thorn whispered in her ear. "He's in a bad way."

She didn't answer. At all. Her deep, even breathing told him what had happened.

A moment later, Cam confirmed it. "She's asleep. Leave her be."

"What about you?" Thorn frowned.

"You offering to help me?" With a grimace, Cam began to stroke his long length in slow motions. The pad of his thumb led the slow stroke up the inches of his cock, pressing into the sensitive spot where the shaft and the head joined before gliding back down.

Thorn could barely tear his gaze away. It was another guy, stroking his own meat. Normally, that would be just fucking nasty to him. But something about watching Cam leisurely ramp up his pleasure was getting to him. Already his own dick was starting to stir.

"Like you helped me?" He injected a sneer in his voice.

"Like that."

"Dude, you're making a move on me?"

Cam lifted his huge, muscled shoulders in a shrug. "She's asleep, and doing this shit to yourself isn't that fun... You're the only other person here."

He sounded so casual, like it was no big deal to him whether another guy touched his dick or not. Then again, to him, maybe it wasn't.

"Are you gay?"

Cameron laughed and rolled his eyes. "No. I'm open-minded."

Now what the hell did that mean? He swung both ways? "You ever fucked a guy?"

"Once." No hesitation, no looking away, no embarrassment. "In college."

Thorn was weirded out by the answer. He was, right? Of course. For the most part. But another part of him... "If it was only once, it must have been awful."

"I'd be lying if I said I didn't enjoy it. It was just different." Again, he shrugged, still stroking his cock. "I was into women and still am. I was just curious to see how the other team played."

Thorn tried not to be distracted, tried to focus just on what Cam was saying, but the sight of that hand slowly, slowly stroking his cock was hard to look away from.

"But you never did it again?"

"Haven't had the right opportunity, right person. I might never have that again. I love women, so it's cool."

He loved women too. If he had his way, women would always be like a glass of water to him—six to eight a day for good health. Yet watching Cam rub a thumb over the purple head of his dick and soothe the long shaft in his broad palm over and over had him hard once more.

What the hell was wrong with him? Until this moment, he'd never thought about how the other team played, and he didn't want to play for them now. But Cam made him just a little bit curious…

Suddenly, the detective tensed, shuddered, moaned. He picked up speed, his hand rubbing his length faster, his palm gripping tighter.

Thorn was glued to the show. Brenna shifted in his lap, and he absently petted her back and hip as she slept. But he wasn't hard because he had his arms full of sated woman. It was all the visual spectacle of Cam masturbating.

"The idea doesn't repulse you," Cam asserted with a pointed glance at Thorn's hard cock.

He followed that by savage strokes of his hand over his flesh. The head turned more purple. Cam's breathing hitched. The muscles of his thighs stood out. He was getting closer, Thorn knew. And still he couldn't look away.

"It should. Normally, it would."

"But you want to see me come." It wasn't a question.

Thorn's arms tightened around Brenna. He hesitated, not wanting to answer. In his head, he heard the Final Jeopardy music. Cam was waiting for an answer.

With the last mental *boing*, Thorn blurted, "Yeah."

"I'm private," Cam whispered. "Normally I wouldn't do this. But sharing Brenna made everything different for me. I don't think we're done with her."

Or necessarily with each other.

The unspoken words hung in the air.

A hot chill raced up Thorn's spine. He was terrified, horny and weirded out all at once. But the overload of emotions wasn't enough to stop the freight train from barreling down the track.

"Finish it. I want to watch."

Cam gave him a shaky nod, then his fist began pounding his cock. His biceps flexed, the veins in his hand stood out as his cock swelled and his balls drew up to his body. Those Native American cheekbones flushed with arousal. The little buttons of his nipples drew up into tight pinpoints.

Without thinking, Thorn reached out and scraped the bud of his finger over Cam's nipple.

As if it was the trigger for a cataclysm, Cam's head jerked back and he let out a massive roar. Hot seed jetted out, spilling all over his thighs.

And for some reason, that was one of the most mesmerizing things Thorn had ever witnessed. What the hell was that about?

* * * * *

Brenna woke to the sun midway up the morning sky and a blanket tucked around her on the sofa. She blinked, sat up. Cam's house. She let out a relieved breath. *Safe.*

The detective shuffled half dressed around the kitchen. God, he was incredible to look at. Dark and poster-worthy, bronze skin over the rippling, well-worked muscle of his back, that nearly black hair just brushing the tops of his bulging shoulders... He made her wet just standing there, his biceps visibly flexing as he fried bacon. The scene was so domestic, yet he would never be strictly domesticated.

But it wasn't just his appearance that drew her. Last night, she'd glimpsed his understanding, felt the care in his touch. The exterior might be badass detective, and he, no doubt, intimidated his fair share of criminals, but under all that was a really decent guy. He wasn't the kind of man who would father a child and leave her on his sister's doorstep, never to return. He not only shouldered responsibility, he took it completely onto his back without so much as a shrug. Maybe that's what she'd responded to last night, what had allowed her to orgasm.

She swallowed. "Can I help?"

He sent her a smile—the real deal—eyes crinkling in the corners. "Sit. You already cooked breakfast once, which no one got to eat. I'll see if we fare better with brunch."

A sound behind her alerted her, and she whipped her gaze around. Thorn emerging from the master bathroom, freshly showered. Bare-chested, he was also drool worthy. Powerful golden shoulders undulating, abs rippling, with every swipe of his towel through his damp hair, Thorn was totally male. He didn't just wear a don't-fuck-with-me mantle, he *epitomized* it. And yet...those little glimpses of tenderness peeked through.

"You okay, baby?"

Brenna nodded, feeling tears sting her eyes.

Since she'd fallen asleep on his lap, she was certain he'd been the one to cover her with the cozy blanket. Normally, she hated being called baby, but something about the way he said it now... He wasn't immune to her, just like she wasn't to him. But he screamed temporary. She had little doubt that the time they had left together could be measured in hours, yet her body had willingly come for him. Why?

Being with the guys was breaking down the tough-girl barriers she'd erected to protect her heart and revealing her soft underside she couldn't hide from them. Thorn needed her tenderness, and she couldn't not respond to Cam with utter emotional honesty.

If she wasn't careful, she was going to fall for them.

With the two of them sandwiching her, she felt protected. They'd proved they would take care of her this morning, saving her from the would-be abductors. Men after her because they wanted to know where her father was. Because they wanted to kill him? She had a million questions and almost no answers.

"Chow is ready," Cameron called.

As he passed the couch, Thorn held out his hand to her.

Brenna took it and got to her feet, meeting the direct stare he leveled her way. Something was going on in his head, but she couldn't tell exactly what from his weighty expression. He'd be a hard one to get to spill his secrets, she'd bet. He'd have to trust, and like her, she'd bet he didn't do that easily.

It was crazy to hope that, someday, he would feel free to tell her anything…everything. But she still hoped as she placed her hand in his and squeezed.

"I could swear I have a hole in my stomach." Thorn's belly rumbled on cue, and he rubbed a huge hand over his ribbed abdomen. "You wear me out, baby."

Ditto in double for her. Despite this morning's scare, every limb in her body felt loose, every muscle relaxed.

Hand in hand, she and Thorn made their way to the table. Cam pulled out a chair, and when she approached it, he drew his arm around her and bent to her, pressing a sweet, lingering kiss to her mouth. Warmth glowed inside her at the casual ease of his affection. What would it be like to have someone so clearly caring in her life who wasn't a blood relative and didn't love you because they felt obligated?

Behind her, Thorn's hand tightened on hers. He edged closer. Shockingly, he was hard again. Cam sidled closer and nudged her lips apart with his own. She stood on her tiptoes to throw her arms around his neck. Surprise, surprise. She could feel his erection beneath the loose gray sweatpants he'd donned.

Someone massaged her back, rubbing their way down with soothing strokes until they cupped her ass. Cam. Thorn was busy working his hands around her waist, up her rib cage…and fondling her breasts with their sore little nipples. They weren't the only thing sore, and, what do you know? She was getting wet anyway.

Talk about an alternate universe. For someone who hadn't bothered with men and sex in years, suddenly she'd gorged on two—and apparently wasn't sated yet. She'd had a bad-girl reputation in high school for sleeping around, looking for that elusive orgasm. But she'd never really lived up to that reputation until now.

Thorn gave her nipple another brush and whispered against her neck. "I've never had to make such a tough choice between my belly and my dick."

Cam laughed. "Let's eat before it gets cold."

Brenna sat, Thorn beside her, and Cam brought bacon, hash browns, fresh fruit, eggs and tortillas. He set a jar of salsa in the middle of the table.

She stared at it, then at him. "What's that for?"

"Breakfast burritos." The detective smiled, showing a dimple in one cheek. "Everything's better with salsa."

"Yeah, if you want to burn your taste buds off before noon," Thorn quipped. "I've eaten lunch with this guy before. If the food doesn't make him sweat, he's not happy."

"Scandinavian-bred pussy won't even try the salsa."

Thorn suggested to Cam that he try something both trite and anatomically impossible.

As they all dug in and began to eat, questions began to whirl through her head. Where was her father? He had to be alive, or the goons this morning wouldn't have come for her. But what sort of trouble was he in? He'd been offered immunity for his testimony, Cam had said. But what black things had he done?

The guys were silent, slaves to shoving in calories. Brenna knew she should eat a few more bites, suspecting—and hoping—she'd need the energy later.

"What's wrong?" Cam asked between enormous bites of food.

"Those men this morning…they want to kill my father."

Cam hesitated, shot Thorn a glance. Brenna noticed that the bounty hunter gave a quick nod.

He nodded back. "You should know what you're up

against. Your father worked for Julio Marco. They were in the business of smuggling in illegal aliens across the Mexico-Arizona border, then turning into slaves."

"I got that from the paper, but slaves? Real-life slaves?"

"Anything from servants, to sweatshop workers to prostitutes."

"My father promised these people safe passage across the border, then imprisoned them and forced them to…" Horror seeped through her. What kind of man did that make him? Then again, what kind of man abandoned his baby by leaving her with a woman she'd never met?

Cam laid a hand over hers. "I know he smuggled them in and he knew, at least roughly, what was happening after that. But exactly, no. Marco wouldn't allow that. He's the ringleader and the asshole we really want behind bars. Your father is just a hired gun who paid attention. He has critical information, and when I arrested him, he promised to sing like a bird if we cut him slack. The State District Attorney agreed to the deal, we took his sworn statement, and we told him to lie low. I'm not supposed to know this but the Feds were talking about Witness Protection, so I'm thinking he made them the same deal."

And the trial started in five days. Brenna swallowed.

"Before all the deals were done, he called me to bail his ass out of jail," Thorn groused. "I need to find him. I'm not interested in being out fifty K. My brother told me not to take his bond…"

"I can't look all the victims of this scam in the eye if I don't bring your dad into testify. I promised them justice, and I can't not deliver."

"Can you help us find him, baby?"

After hearing the vile things her father had been up to, she didn't think she owed him silence. He'd warned her about dirty cops being after him, but Cam was no more a dirty cop than she was a lumberjack.

"Like I said before, all I have is a cell phone number. He never answers it. I always leave a message. Sometimes he calls back…"

Sometimes he didn't. With their grim nods, it was clear Cam and Thorn got the message.

"Would you try him now?" Cam asked. "I think you should tell him that some of his friends tried to force you to go with them for an involuntary visit."

Brenna hesitated then nodded. She hated calling Curtis. But to help Cam and Thorn, and all of her father's victims, she'd do it twenty times over.

Quickly, she retrieved her purse and dug out her cell phone. Sure enough, after four rings, the voicemail took over. It was stupid to hope that one day he'd answer the phone and be happy to hear from her. Somehow, the electronic voice leaving her voicemail instructions always depressed her.

After the beep, she told her dad about the morning's danger, indicated that she was with Cameron, and asked for a call back.

As soon as she flipped the phone shut, she looked up to find Cam staring at her with traces of pity. Thorn looked like he was suppressing a healthy dose of anger.

"I'm sorry I can't just…produce him," she defended, rising from her chair.

Truth was, she was a little hurt by Thorn's silent accusation. True, he wasn't the most sensitive guy on the planet, but for him to basically blame her…

As she walked away from the table, a strong grip clapped around her arm and tugged her back. With a *whoomp*, she fell back into Thorn's lap.

Anger churning through her, she flashed a glare at him, itching for a fight. Instead, his face was contrite.

"Baby, I'm not mad at you. I'm mad *for* you. I know a thing or two about shitty fathers."

A personal comment from Thorn? Even Cameron looked mildly surprised that he'd divulged something about himself.

"What?" Thorn defended. "I may come off like an asshole but I'm not completely heartless. When you look at me with those doe eyes, a heartbeat from tears, I'm as human as the next guy."

Brenna curled up on his lap and brushed a soft kiss across his mouth.

"Tell me why you came to visit him," Cam asked, observing Thorn kiss her neck and palm her ass.

It should be weird to be touching one of her lovers while the other watched. Oddly, it seemed like the most normal thing in the world.

"I actually came out here to...figure Curtis out. Figure us out. My problem..." She blushed.

"Which doesn't seem to be much of a problem with us." Thorn grinned and popped a piece of cantaloupe in his mouth.

Brenna's cheeks grew hotter. "No, it doesn't. But the issue caused me to lose a fiancé. Tony was a great guy, and I..." She shrugged. "I was clingy and convinced he was going to leave. About six months ago, he did, and I was crushed but not surprised. After that, I started really thinking about my life. I read some self-help books, talked to a friend. And I realized my dad's departure from my life was hanging me up in a lot of ways, but especially sexually."

"Your ex's loss is our gain, and I don't want you to worry. We're not going anywhere anytime soon."

"At least until my father shows up."

Cameron stood and towered above her. Brenna looked up, up, up until she met his solemn dark eyes.

"I'm not sure that changes anything for me. When I first met you, you got under my skin right away. After last night...you've only managed to sink deeper. I'm in no hurry to leave."

She tried not to gape at him. "But last night, we... I... I mean, both of you, and—"

"Yes, you made love with both of us last night and again this morning. Are you going to try to tell me that you have no sense of connection to us?"

And be honest? "No. I just never expected... I never imagined that you'd share my feelings."

He smiled and stroked her hair. "You're damn hard to resist. The woman who met me at the door, gun in hand, after beating the stuffing out of a punching bag showed me a needy side that night we watched you by the pool. Last night, we saw your tenacious side, your sexual side, when you trusted us with your body. And just now, you showed your vulnerable, trusting side when you told us about your relationship with your father. You don't hide yourself, and I love it."

Cameron's words slid so sweet through her, intoxicating like good champagne. Everything was happening so fast, and the cautious woman who'd stepped off the plane a few days ago had been stripped bare—literally and figuratively. Her emotions split open, her sexuality tested like never before. She felt both free and terrified. What happened now?

"You surprised me too," she admitted. "Cop with an attitude one minute, the male version of Dr. Ruth the next." She turned to Thorn. "You, too. Mr. Badass Biker. When you call me 'baby' the way you do, I hear your inner teddy bear. You covered me with the blanket earlier, didn't you?"

Thorn didn't reply. Instead, the line of his jaw tensed—just like the shoulders beneath her hands. *Uh oh.*

"I know you don't want me to care, but—"

"I don't. I want to fuck. You and the good detective can continue your love fest after the condom is off, I've zipped my pants and found the door."

She'd known it was coming, just by the look on his face. She searched those blue eyes so like a frozen Scandinavian lake. He wasn't annoyed or unmoved or offended. Lurking deep in his eyes was fear.

Brenna had to bite her lip not to reassure him. He wasn't in a place where he could be cajoled now. It took time to develop trust, and she'd bet someone had burned him bad. Caring and time— She stopped the thought. Time was the one thing they didn't have much of.

Five days, that's all she and Cam had to win Thorn over. *If* he hung around that long.

Why winning him over mattered, she didn't know. Technically, she was supposed to get on a plane and return home in a handful of days. Her life, such as it was, was back in Muenster. Her waitressing job awaited. True, it was a job she hated and she made lousy money…

Brenna sighed. Well, her aunt and cousins were the only family she had beyond Curtis. Leaving them… Would be no big deal. She'd lived with them since childhood but had never been a part of them. No matter how they tried to integrate her into their tight-knit clan, she'd always known she wasn't one of them. Was infringing. Sponging. The older she'd gotten, the more aware of it she'd become.

Last Christmas had been excruciating. Her aunt glowing in the face of her three married sons, two of them with wives expecting, had been heaven and hell. She was happy for Josh, Bryan and Billy. They were great guys who deserved all the best. Every time the family gathered, their happiness just underscored her only deficiencies. She was an unintentional afterthought, and that reality was nails to her chalkboard.

What did she really have to go back to? Not her superficial friendships. Not her run-down apartment. Nothing.

Did she dare try to turn this stress-induced affair with Cam and Thorn into something more permanent? Good question. An even better question was, would she be miserable if she didn't try and just went home to her nothing life, always wonder what if?

Absolutely.

But what if Thorn couldn't be swayed? What if his heart had been too damaged by whatever haunted him? It was possible. He'd looked way more terrified of his own emotional vulnerability than the goons with the guns this morning. Maybe the smartest thing would be to stay with just Cam. When it came to matters of the heart, she and Cam seemed to be on the same page.

But without Thorn, it wouldn't be the same. She was probably crazy to contemplate scheming her way into a relationship with two men. It would always be complicated. Her aunt and cousins would never approve. She didn't care. Her gut told her she'd be happy.

First, she had to conquer Thorn's fear.

Her aunt had always said that the quickest way to a man's heart was either through his stomach—or his penis. She was great in the kitchen and gaining confidence in the bedroom. Thorn was going to get to see how much.

It was definitely time for a plan.

Chapter Nine

ഔ

Brenna swallowed, lifted her chin, sent him a proud glare before turning to Cameron beside him. "I'm going to grab a shower, if that's okay."

Thorn resisted the urge to wince when Cam shot him a nasty glower, then reached out to cup her shoulder in tender concern. "Sure. There are towels stacked up on the counter. Plenty of shampoo and soap. Lotion is under the sink, if you want some after your bath. As my father's people always said, '*Mi casa es su casa.*'"

"Thanks. I'll make myself at home. Temporarily. I don't want to intrude for long."

Cam opened his mouth to rebut her but Brenna had already gone, her shoulders in a dejected set, long hair brushing the small of her back.

As soon as a soft *snick* revealed the door shut behind her, Cam turned to him with a look that could have melted diamonds. So the even-tempered detective had a temper. Fine time to find that out... Aw, hell. It didn't matter what Cam said. Thorn didn't think he could feel any worse than he'd already made himself feel.

"Don't say it," he warned Cam.

"Oh, I'm not only going to say it, I'm going to carve it into your forehead, prick. Did you hear yourself? 'I want to fuck. You and the good detective can continue your love fest after the condom is off, I've zipped my pants and found the door.'" Cam's voice dripped incredulity. "Could you make her feel any more like a whore? She's spent her whole adult life having trouble climaxing because Curtis hurt her and she feared abandonment, then you announce you're going to leave her in the most crass way possible. She all but tells you that she cares about you, and you crap all over her and tell her she's just a fuck?" Cam backed up. "Unreal, asshole. Totally unreal.

"I'll take care of her from here on out," Cam went on. "I'll call you when we find Curtis. You can take him in and get your money and go back to sleeping with a different woman every other night until you're too old to attract a woman or catch some damn disease. Either way, you're going to die alone, and clearly, you want it that way. Guess what? I'm going to help you. Get the hell out."

The detective turned to leave.

Stunned and silent, Thorn stared. Cam had always been somewhere between understanding and easygoing. Thorn knew he was high-strung and came off like a motherfucker. He didn't mean it, exactly. Mostly he didn't give a shit about anything or anyone. But when he did… Well, he didn't really know how to deal with it, much less how to show it. Or worse, how to talk about it.

Trying to dissect your feelings with a crack-addict, drug-dealing father and an absent brother hadn't taught him a lot in the sensitivity department.

The truth was, Brenna did matter. More than he was comfortable saying. Admitting it would give her the power to hurt him, and he liked kink, but pain wasn't his thing. But the thought of leaving her to Cam and never seeing her again—leaving Cam himself—was as welcome as a vise for his balls.

"Wait," he rasped out. "I…" *I what?*

Cam whirled back, and still Thorn didn't know what to say.

"Spit it out," Cam demanded.

But Thorn couldn't. He swallowed, stared, searching for words in a suddenly empty head.

"You want to stay?"

Thorn scowled against a hammer of pain but nodded.

God, Cam could read his mind now too? He hated feeling so damn...inadequate and bottled up. Cam continued to look at him as if he was a lower life form, damn it. It wasn't like he was having a party in his own fucking skin.

With a roar, Thorn turned and punched the nearest door. It hurt like hell, and he shook his fist. But the truth was, he still hurt inside worse.

"You break my door, I don't care. You'll be fixing it. But if you stay and you break her heart, and I swear I'll rip you a new asshole—for starters."

Thorn took a deep breath. Another. There was a beast...something very angry that was awake and running amok inside him. He'd fucked up, he knew it. What he didn't know was how to fix it. It frustrated him to fury.

"I don't want to break her heart, damn it. I... She started talking about feelings and shit. A part of me was happy, you know? The other part is just... Aw, hell. I panicked. I gave her my standard answer whenever any woman gives me the 'I want monogrammed towels' look. Truth is..." He shuffled his feet, took in a deep breath and went for broke. "I could be with you two more. I wanna be. But I suck at relationships."

"People get close and you get scared you might have to let someone see the real you, that you might have to be reliable for someone. That you might have to give yourself." Cam's eyes narrowed. "You're afraid of true intimacy."

Bingo. Damn Cam. Perceptive son of a bitch. Dissecting his hang-ups was somewhere between uncomfortable and having a dozen rusty nails hammered into his dick.

"And your point is?" he quipped. Telling Cam he was right would only make Thorn feel worse.

"If you want to stay, fix it. Learn how to be honest about your wants and feelings with yourself and us. Otherwise, get the hell out. But decide what you want before Brenna is out of the shower, because I'm not letting you anywhere near her again unless you promise not to hurt her. She's a one-of-a-kind woman who deserves more than a fuck and run."

After that little speech, Cam turned and walked toward the master bedroom and Brenna, shutting the door behind him. The detective had been a good guy, which, Thorn supposed, earned him the right to watch the water slide over her soft, pale curves. Maybe help her out of the shower, towel her off, then do whatever he damn well pleased.

While Thorn...he'd be standing here with his dick in his hand and alone for freaking ever if he didn't get his shit figured out in a hurry.

"Hell." Thorn rubbed the back of his neck.

Why didn't Cam just ask him to bend over and take an enema? It wouldn't be any less personal. Of course, the bastard was also right.

Leaving was tempting but not an option he wanted to take. He liked what he'd found here with Brenna and Cam more than he didn't want to endure the pain that would come later. Normally, confronted with this shit, he'd inhale twelve beers, head to a strip club and pick up Ms. Right-for-the-night. Or go crack a few skulls when bringing in the bail-jumping trash to Tucson's finest. But neither of these ideas were going to help him confront his inner demons.

Which only left him one option—he was going to have to rip off the scab and hope he didn't bleed to death.

* * * * *

Cam eased open the door to the bathroom and called in, "Everyone indecent?"

"Come in," Brenna called as she shut the shower door, towel wrapped around her wet hair—and everything else bare as the day she was born.

"Damn, I'm too late. I was going to offer to wash every square inch of your body with soap. Twice at least."

She sent him a soft smile and wrapped another towel

around her body, but Cam could see she was still upset, and none of his lame joking was going to undo the hurt of Thorn's mean-spirited words.

Seeing her here in his bedroom, in his kitchen, napping on his sofa all seemed so…natural, it was unnerving. But he liked it. A lot. And hoped like hell that Thorn's standoffish crap hadn't made her skittish.

"What a swell offer." She grabbed his hands and put them around her waist, doing her best to put on an unaffected act, though he knew Thorn had emotionally bruised her. "Want to practice now, sans soap?"

Cam eased his gun onto the nightstand, then wrapped his arms around her waist and drew her against his body. She was a little thing, all of five feet two or three. Probably weighed around one ten. But in that little body was such a big heart. How many people in her situation would have gone to a therapist and paid *beaucoup* money to learn to tell their father to fuck off? Instead, she came back to the very man who'd hurt her to try to understand him, to get to know him. And after being dumped by her fiancé, she didn't give up on love either. She just kept going, not pausing to lick her wounds. Cam respected that, loved that about her.

"I'm never going to turn that offer down."

Her sunny smile went straight between his pecs, piercing deep…and a bit lower. The latter didn't surprise him. But feeling her in his chest was a stunner. His grandmother had always told him that someday he'd fall in love quickly and irrevocably. It was the way of his mother's people. But the Apache were a superstitious lot, steeped in some old beliefs, despite the fact they loved technology. His father's people…they just married and had babies like mad. But his parents were still happily married and living in Albuquerque. They'd made an interracial marriage work, so…

Where the hell was this thought going? He'd met Brenna one day ago and the "M" word had already entered his brain?

"Now is a good time," Brenna said, bringing him out of his reverie. "If you're not going to turn it down, that is."

"Yes, ma'am." He ran his palm down her back, then edged his hand up under the towel to cup her ass.

She cuddled against him, and it just felt right. Or mostly right. But something was missing.

As he skated soft kisses across her neck and let his free hand roam her skin, Cam knew that it wasn't something missing, but some*one*.

Damn Thorn!

"I'm sorry about the things Thorn said, and I hope you don't—"

"I'll do my own apologizing, Cop."

Brenna gasped, and Cam whirled. In the doorway, Thorn stood looking both tense and arrogantly male.

Cam resisted the urge to smile. He honestly hadn't believed Thorn would come around. The bounty hunter ran through women faster than a gallon of water through his taps. *If* Thorn came around, Cam had never expected it to be this quick. Maybe that meant he was hooked more than anyone suspected.

At least Cam hoped so.

Until Brenna had come along and they'd spent their first night as a trio, Cam had never noticed Thorn as anything but a bounty hunter and pseudo-friend. But now... He hadn't been attracted to another guy since college. What he felt now was a complicated mix of curiosity, anger and pity. There were layers to Thorn and a lot of hurt, Cam suspected. But no way was he letting Thorn stay here if he intended to use the sex to hide.

He'd wait to hear what the bounty hunter had to say, but if it was another load of bullshit, Thorn was going to feel the door on his ass. If he said the right things...well, Cam had a plan to make sure that what was inside Thorn's heart backed them up.

* * * * *

"I'm sorry, baby." Thorn stood in the bedroom doorway and looked down as he shuffled his feet. His heart knocked against his ribs like a woodpecker with a fresh tree. "I'm no good with words of feelings. Lack of practice. But, um... You're not just a fuck to me. I've had enough of them to know the difference. I wanna keep you safe but it's more than that. And I...have no idea what else to say."

Brenna slipped from Cam's embrace, took his hand, and led him to Thorn's side. He tensed as they neared. She was totally within her rights to slap him. If their positions were reversed, he'd beat the shit out of himself.

Not Brenna. The woman dragged him into the middle of the bedroom and brushed a soft kiss over his mouth, her small hand gliding over his bare shoulder in gentle understanding. Damn, everything about her amazed him.

"I know what it's like to be afraid to be hurt again. I don't know who or what happened to you, and you don't have to tell me until you're ready. But I want you to know that I'm nothing but honest. I care about you and I will never hurt you on purpose."

Holy shit. Under her touch, her words, Thorn tensed. He closed his eyes, drew in a deep, shuddering breath, trying to regain control. It was either that, or bawl like a goddamn baby. Tears jabbed at the back of his eyes like a pickaxe. He wanted to throw his arms around her, beg forgiveness, then spend half the night inside her. But he didn't dare indulge in his last wish. He hadn't earned the right. And Thorn suspected that if he tried, he and Cam would argue again.

Finally getting his shit under control, he met her soft stare and caressed her cheek. "That means a lot to me, baby. I'm a bastard by nature, but I'll try not to lash out when I'm uptight or whatever. You, um...matter. I didn't mean to hurt you."

"I know." She smiled.

Thorn wanted to ask how she knew but didn't. Maybe it

was a woman thing or a been-there-done-that thing. Whatever it was, he was grateful.

"But this isn't just about me," she said. "I think you two had words, probably some harsh ones. You have to work together after I'm gone, so you need to bury the hatchet." Brenna stepped aside and pulled Cam closer.

The cop was big and dark and smelled like danger in a way that made his heart pump. Thorn didn't want to call the reaction sexual, but he'd be lying if he didn't admit there was a bit of that in the mix. At the moment, he admired the hell out of Cam's honesty with himself. Thorn knew he needed to learn that, not flinch every time he had an emotion. It wasn't like his old man was going to be here to mock him or beat the shit out of him for it.

"Sorry, man." He extended his hand. "You got nothing to apologize for except being right all the damn time."

Cam took his hand, and Thorn felt a weird jolt of attraction. God, he'd never really looked at guys. He'd always been about women since his first at thirteen. But this wasn't sex. Thorn couldn't break this down, but it was complicated. A bit of respect, a bond of friendship, a jolt of sexual zing—and still more he couldn't classify.

The detective tugged on his hand, pulling him in until their bare chests collided. Cam's arm came around his shoulders until he clapped him on the back. Thorn returned the gesture. Something both glad and forbidden streaked through his blood.

Oh, fuck. He'd gone hard. Thorn gritted this teeth. Now what?

Cam backed away slowly. Thorn tried to keep his gaze just on Brenna, standing beside Cam. But the cop's heavy gaze compelled him, and Thorn felt his stare creep over to those dark eyes. Knowing eyes. Sexual eyes.

Cam knew he was hard and was aroused by it?

Thorn drew in a deep breath. *Flow with it. It's nobody's*

business what you do in the bedroom but yours.

Brenna approached them both and wrapped her arms around their waists. She pressed a quick kiss to Cam's mouth then turned to him.

"Feel better?"

Oddly, he did. Usually others…he really didn't give a shit. Cam was the closest thing to a friend he'd had in years. And Brenna, with her kind hazel eyes, was impossible not to adore. But it wasn't just them. A sense of belonging seeped under his skin and into his bones. That itchy, restless feeling that usually dogged him after he fucked a woman and lingered more than a three minutes was remarkably absent.

"Yeah."

A smile broke out across her face, and her arm tightened around his waist as she leaned in and placed a sweet kiss on his mouth. "I'm glad."

"Do you have bounties to catch today?" Cam asked.

He shrugged. "Lars can handle it. I went on a tear last week, so I'm pretty caught up. He can handle whatever is outstanding. That's what older brothers are for."

"Call him and make sure. I think we need to hang loose in case Curtis calls back. I have a feeling that whatever happens next is going to be fast."

Thorn nodded and grabbed the phone at this belt, punching numbers as he drifted out the door. In a few short words, he'd arranged a day to do nothing but lie low.

He stepped back into the bedroom to see Cam pressing whispery kisses on Brenna's cheek, jaw, neck, his bronze skin brushing over her milky paleness. The sight of them was an adrenaline shot to his dick.

Damn if he didn't want to join them. Now.

"You cool?" Cam asked, barely dragging his mouth away from Brenna and turning her in his arms so he could rub his palms over her delicate shoulders.

Just a little lower, and Cam could be dissolving that towel from her body and fondling her breasts...and he could be watching and salivating and hoping he got the chance to taste heaven too.

But he did his best to play cool. Business first. "Lars agreed that fifty K was more than enough money to justify giving the bond my all. So I'm dedicated to it for the next day or two."

"Good. Today is my day off, technically. So I can use the time to wait with you and see if Curtis emerges. The clock is ticking, but I've figured out that if we try to hunt him down, he'll just dig deeper into his hidey-hole."

"Especially if he knows someone is trying to kill him."

"And he'd be an idiot to think Marco isn't trying to off him as quickly as possible."

"Damn straight," Thorn agreed. "And if there's one thing Curtis isn't..."

"It's stupid." Cam nodded, brushing a long caress down Brenna's arm, then back up to her collarbone. "He knows that testifying and Witness Protection are his best bets to stay alive. I wish he'd allowed us to provide protective custody, but the minute Judge Nelson granted him bail, I suspected he'd go deep."

The sight of Cam's hands on Brenna was damn distracting. "With someone like Marco chasing you, wouldn't you?"

"Likely."

"How did my father get involved in all this?" Brenna asked. "It's not like we have a deep relationship, but I never imagined him to be a criminal."

"I don't know." Cam shook his head. "Curtis wasn't that talkative when I questioned him. He answered what was asked directly but didn't offer more. I didn't ask why. If I had to guess, though, it's like everyone else. The lure of the easy money is just too strong."

Brenna recoiled. "It's so ugly. These are *people*, for goodness sake."

"Some people look at other people and see nothing but dollar signs, baby." Thorn grabbed her and rubbed a soothing thumb over the back. "It is ugly, but Cam and I see the dregs of society every day. It's nothing new for us."

"Vice is a regular barrel of fun," Cam drawled.

She shuddered. "Back in my little town in Texas, the most dangerous character I ever saw was the occasional handsy guy who'd come to the diner and think a free feel came with his mashed potatoes."

Her words exploded an instant picture into Thorn's head of some unwashed creep putting his hands on Brenna's ass, and he tensed, wishing he had heads to knock around. He didn't like the thought of her having to fend off these assholes on her own.

"Know how to break their fingers?"

She sent him a chastising glance. "Violence against customers would be bad for business."

"But better for my mental health. Be careful, baby."

She sidled closer and snuggled up to him and laid her head on his chest. "With you here, I feel completely safe."

That suddenly, he felt both a hundred feet tall and invisible ties winding around his heart.

Shit, was he hooked? Was love that quick and simple? And what about Cam?

He slanted a glance at the detective, who didn't look at all unhappy that he had his arm around Brenna's waist while his fingers removed the towel covering her long honey-brown hair. In fact, that sleepy, sensual expression on the detective's face conveyed anything but anger.

This whole sharing a woman thing… Looking at Cam's face, he didn't think the cop saw it as an isolated event or two. Mentally, Thorn tried on the idea of making this a relationship.

Immediately, blood rushed south, pulsing, making his dick throb insistently.

Okay, so that part of him dug it. Shocker... If history repeated, he knew the sex would never be anything but astounding. But there were practical reasons too. Brenna would always be protected. She'd never feel unloved or abandoned again. If he begged or fucked appropriately, there might be some home-cooked meals in his future. And this warm, gooey feeling in his chest that made him weirdly happy might stay. He could be important, not just to one person, but two. He might actually feel like his personal life had meaning beyond orgasms with strangers.

At thirty-three, he finally wanted more than a one-night stand with someone whose name he couldn't remember. Maybe even something to last.

"You are completely safe," Thorn assured her, tugging gently on her damp hair to tip her head back. He looked straight into those hazel eyes and swore he could see forever as he lowered his mouth to hers.

Soft, like a cotton blanket on a warm bed — that's how she felt against him. Petal-sweet lips parted under his, and he dove deep, sinking into oblivion. And he didn't care. There was something here he'd never felt anywhere else. He wasn't about to let her get away.

Even with his eyes closed, he felt a sudden surge of heat near Brenna. Cam. The detective pressed himself against her backside and wrapped his hands around her waist. He caressed slowly, palms rising to her breasts, dragging his knuckles across her nipples. She groaned into Thorn's mouth. That, coupled with the soft abrasion of the back of Cam's fingers caressing his torso, juiced his blood in a flash.

Thorn's kiss turned from an affirmation to a conquering in the span of a heartbeat as he turned on the heat. Under him, Brenna melted. Then an unexpected touch as Cam's fingers brushed his shoulder, sending electricity straight to his dick. The touch drifted away and returned to Brenna but the effect lingered.

Just from that, Thorn suspected Cam was going to push his boundaries. And instead of being freaked, he was feeling very *bring it on*. Quickly, he laid his gun on the dresser just a lunge away from where he currently stood, just in case. Then the turned back to the others.

Brenna removed her hands from Thorn's body, and before he could protest, she tugged at the towel around her body, baring herself to them. Thorn took advantage of the sudden access to soft skin and glided his palms over her back and downward.

The backs of his fingers brushed the thick ridge of Cam's erection on the way down.

The detective hissed, and Thorn smiled inwardly. *Take that.* Then he focused on Brenna's prime ass, trailing his fingers over her cheeks, between her legs, between her lips. He smiled. Wet. Just the way he wanted her.

Easing his fingers inside her, she closed around him silky hot and tight. She was going to be a delight for his dick. And Cam's. The thought of both of them sharing one pussy should have pissed him off, grossed him out—something. Nope. He was so jacked on desire, he was a step from throwing her to the bed, tearing off his jeans and working his cock straight in.

But he wanted to draw it out, make her scream and beg…and see whether Cam would contribute to her sensual torture or succumb to the towering need to fuck her immediately.

Cam continued to toy with her nipples, pinching, turning, sensitizing. Brenna's little moans were eating at his resolve. And when Cam sank passionate kisses across her shoulder, then up her neck, to her lobe, Thorn felt his heat, the jagged need in his exhalation.

Fingertips brushed down his chest, full of electric sizzle. Brenna's? Cameron's? Did it matter?

He groaned and clutched Brenna tighter, his fingers

pressing into her soft flesh as he slanted his mouth in a new direction to delve deeper into the kiss.

The live wire touch kept drifting lower, stopping at the waistband of his pants. A tug, a jerk of the material, then the jeans sagged away from his waist. The fingers continued, easing down his zipper. Slowly, so damn slowly it was all he could do not to growl at whoever to hurry the fuck up. His dick was like an insistent toothache, refusing to ease up. Pressure was building in his balls. With his fingers still inside Brenna, he knew she was growing tighter, wetter, and all Thorn could think of was getting inside to ease his ache and feel her flesh all round him rippling in release. And Cam watching.

Brenna broke from the kiss and began to trail her open mouth over his shoulder, his chest, until she latched around one of his nipples. She sucked, and the sensation was like fire-laced lightning. He threw his head back, gritted his teeth, and tried to hang onto his self-control.

"Feel good?" Cam asked, his voice low and rough.

"Fuck yeah."

Cam chuckled. Thorn wasn't remotely tempted to join in, especially when the hand tugging down his zipper finally succeeded and pushed his jeans and underwear down around his hips. Cool air wrapped around his cock.

Followed by a hand. A large hand. A firm hand.

A man's hand.

As much as Thorn wanted to deny that it felt good, he couldn't, not when liquid heat shot down his spine, into his balls, broiling him. Then the hand stroked up his shaft, thumb brushing over the head, and he nearly lost it.

"What the fuck are you doing?" Thorn groaned.

"Watching you fight the urge to come." Cam didn't say that he found it sexy, but his voice said it for him.

Knowing he was affecting Cam just imploded Thorn's self-control that much more. His mind railed. He should be revolted. He definitely didn't go for guys, had never once felt an attraction to one he even remotely wanted to heed. But Cam stroked down to the root of Thorn's erection then brushed over his balls. *Amazing.* Thorn moaned long and low.

All rational thought stopped except it felt good, so what the fuck?

Suddenly, Brenna gasped. "Oh my...wow."

"Are you watching me touch Thorn?" Cam asked, stroking back up Thorn's dick.

The sensations were heaping one on the other, overwhelming, earth moving. If he couldn't get a grip, he was going to lose it.

"Yes," Brenna answered breathlessly.

"Like it?" Cam challenged.

"Yes."

Brenna's whisper slid across Thorn's skin. This was pleasing her. Arousing her. Thank the gods. If it had repulsed her, Thorn wasn't sure he really could find the will to tell Cam to stop. The detective held him in the palm of his hand—literally.

Thorn had had hand jobs by the hundreds. Usually, getting him to come like this was a long, slow—and frankly boring—process. But he'd never had one so unexpected, never had one from a man. He wasn't sure what the difference was, maybe a more thorough knowledge of male anatomy and a firmer grip, but less than a half-dozen strokes into this and Thorn was so on the verge of losing it.

"Want to undo him together?" Cam asked.

"Can we?" Brenna breathed.

With his free hand, Cam petted Brenna's hair, caressed her shoulder, cupped her breast. "I have no doubt, sweet girl. On your knees. You suck, I'll stroke."

Thorn looked down to see Brenna lowering herself to the carpet and wearing a huge smile.

Why the hell were they trying to unwind him like this, when they had all the control and he had none? What did they want to prove? Crap, he should stop them, should tell them to fuck off.

Instead, Brenna's mouth closed over the tip of his erection and lowered down to Cam's fingers, which still gripped his base tightly. Together, they worked their way back up his shaft.

Oh fucking hell.

That quick, his heart began to pump in his chest, roar in his ears. Their hands elsewhere on him—a brush of Cameron's fingers across his nipples, or Brenna's grip on his ass—was pounding his self-control. The sensations were like a fiery free fall, a jump from ten thousand feet. He plummeted into desire, falling, falling...

As one, Cam and Brenna worked back down his dick, until he felt the head bump the back of her throat and Cam's thumb and finger ring the base in a grip that nearly had him whimpering.

Damn, if they kept this up, he was going to blow everything, all down her sweet little throat. And while he loved a good blowjob—and this would rank as one of the best ever—he wanted to fuck her more. While Cam fucked her too. Where he could exert some control over the situation and make someone else come with him.

"Stop," he croaked.

In response, Brenna eased back and swirled her tongue over the head of his cock. Cam's hand followed, that lethal thumb slicking over the sensitive flesh left wet by her mouth.

"No," Cam whispered.

Fucking bastard! Pressure gripped his balls, soaked in acid pleasure. Damn! Falling into orgasm all by himself while they held all the control scared the shit out of him. Thorn gritted his teeth, trying to stave off the need to come. He might make it another minute or two if he focused on things like the formaldehyde smell of the morgue or the torture of geometry proofs.

"I don't want this," he growled.

Brenna took him deep in her mouth again, her tongue all around him as Cam kept a tight grip on his cock.

Every muscle in his body tensed. This couldn't happen, not him coming alone under their hands while they watched. It was too...intimate. Brenna was down on her knees, and he couldn't reach her pussy in order to make her come. But Cam... He was the instigator of this shit anyway. Saint Cam should suffer as well.

Pushing aside the voice in his head telling him the idea was insane, Thorn grabbed the waistband of Cam's jeans, tore open the buttons, yanked down the zipper, pushed down his underwear and grabbed the guy's cock.

Familiar, yes—the hardness, the silken skin, the heat—but different. Cam was longer, and Thorn's stroke felt like it went on forever before he reached the head of the detective's cock. Yet Cam's was less thick. In some ways, this dick was easier to stroke than his own. Cataloguing the differences was certainly distracting, and as Thorn massaged the head of Cam's erection with a hard press of thumb, the detective groaned long and loud.

His own need eased off now that his attention was wrapped up not in his own ramp up to orgasm, but Cam's. It helped that Cam was too sidetracked to keep stroking his dick. Now if he could convince Brenna to ease off with her sweet mouth. But she just dragged up and down his length like a wet fist sucking the self-control out of him.

Suddenly Cam's hand joined the action again as if he refocused. Thorn doubled his effort, establishing a lightning-fire stroke up and down the detective's cock. But Cam stayed in control.

And the feel of Cam's hard flesh in his hand only aroused Thorn more.

Brenna and Cam worked together again in perfect synch to cover every inch of his erection. She fondled his balls, and the feel of her fingers in uncharted territory set him tipping toward the edge of pleasure.

Cam's grip tightened, his thumb rubbing a sensitive spot just south of the head. Thorn's blood pounded and his body flashed with heat. Brenna's teeth scraped the head. He closed his eyes, fought to hang on...one breath, another, but they just kept coming at him with strokes designed to destroy resistance and sanity.

Brenna moaned around his cock, and Cam cradled his balls in his palm, press-rubbing one finger on a very sensitive spot just beyond.

"Nice try," Cam whispered in his ear.

When had the bastard gotten that close?

"But distracting me won't work. I won't come before you do. Or even with you. I want to feel you come while we touch you."

Brenna's mouth slid down his cock again, her fingernails digging half-moons into his thighs. The stick of pain, along with the erotic confusion, pushed him to heights he'd never been.

But he refused to go before he understood what was going on, damn it.

"Why?" His voice cracked with restraint.

"You need us. If you're not ready to admit that out loud, I want to see your body admit it for you."

The thought that he might need anyone made him sick. When you needed people, they shit on you, took advantage of you, used you.

"No," he ground out long and low and loud.

Brenna eased off his cock and bit the inside of his thigh. "Cam's right. You say I'm more than a lay. Prove it. Give yourself over to me and Cam."

Hell, this was some sort of power play. Some emotional bullshit. With Cam, when wasn't it? And they were asking for his surrender, his soul. Giving in scared the shit out of him.

Yet…he pictured himself at their mercy, not just being stroked by them, but Brenna's lips lovingly brushing his, Cam's hands reverently gliding over his body, and him just standing here and taking it.

He shouldn't like it, couldn't need it—but the vision slammed him and ripped the control from him. Blood raced to his dick, and his heart chugged. Every breath he took, he smelled a mixture of Brenna's floral sweetness and that mysterious something that made Cam unique.

Though he'd squeezed his eyes closed, Thorn could feel the detective exhale, the guy's breathing every bit as harsh as his own. The end was here, fighting it was getting so damn hard. If he couldn't find a way to get his shit together, he was going to come for them, show his vulnerability. *Fucking hell.*

Thorn scrubbed a hand across his face, and smelled Brenna's juice on his fingers. He loved her pussy, and that just aroused him more. Explosion was seconds away now, right on top of him.

"You want to come?" Cam taunted as he palmed his cock with another mind-bending stroke. "You going to give in to us?"

"Fuck." He gritted this teeth. "You."

Cam laughed. "Maybe someday. Right now, I want you to come right in my hand, right in Brenna's mouth. Give us everything so we can feel it."

No matter how much he wanted to repeat his last response, Thorn really couldn't find his voice. Or anything resembling a coherent sentence. He certainly couldn't find any resistance.

The sensual torture was so powerful, it was like being run over by a train. Thorn's chest rose and fell like a bellows. Pleasure broiled his balls. His spine felt like it was quickly melting, and blood ran through his veins as if it was charged with a thousand volts.

But he gritted his teeth and held on. He couldn't afford to be so vulnerable, to show this much of himself. Yes, it was more than sex, but that didn't mean it had to be a soul-baring free-for-all.

Suddenly, Cam's chest brushed his. Thorn latched onto his biceps for support, and could feel it bulging and flexing as Cam worked his cock. Thorn tried to keep a constant effort on Cam's dick, but need shut down his coordination, and he ended up gripping the erection as if it was a lifeline.

Brenna gave another strong suck, lavishing attention on the head of Thorn's cock. His toes curled as he pictured her on her knees, mouth stretched wide to take him.

Then Cam put the nail in his coffin.

The detective leaned in until Thorn felt the man's breath on his neck. He shuddered as a hot chill raced through him, but Cam proved he wasn't done when he nipped at his lobe and whispered, "Come for us."

Brenna licked the side of his shaft, then promised, "We'll catch you."

Thorn couldn't hold back, no matter how much his brain screamed. No matter how dangerous succumbing might be. He wanted to believe in her. In them. Cam wasn't the kind to play head games for the hell of it or blow sunshine up anyone's ass. Brenna had been hurt herself by a dismissive parent. Neither would be intentionally cruel. And unless he didn't want to be alone for the rest of his life, he was going to have to trust someone sometime—even if it scared the shit out of him.

Brenna sucked him deep, and Cam gripped his shoulders and forced him to meet his stare. Dark, sexual, unbreakable. A silent promise. He *would* be there.

Breath rushed in and out of his body, and his skin was on fire. Blood raced like molten lava. The pleasure grew beyond acute. Unbelievable. Bigger not only than anything he'd ever experienced, but bigger than anything he'd ever imagined. Brenna was unhinging his soul. Cam was sucking it in through that compelling stare.

And Thorn chose to let it go.

He gave over the control he'd been clinging to, like a toddler with a favorite blanket. Security was for sissies…and men who'd fucked hundreds of times and never truly been intimate with anyone.

The pleasure was like a towering wave, coming at him, enormous, scary, threatening to drown him. Then it broke over him, and he shouted, electricity charging every cell, every nerve. The sensations drowned him as hot seed erupted from his dick. Brenna's tongue was there to take everything he gave her, and Cam never looked away, the grip on his shoulders always stable, always there.

Ecstasy plowed him flat as the orgasm went on and on. Time, place—gone. Only him and Brenna and Cam in a locked circle of release and support.

Then his legs began to give out. Muscles felt weak and spent, unable to even support him, and he lunged for the bed. He didn't quite make it to the soft mattress, but Cam was there to catch him and help him the extra way. Brenna was right behind, soothing him the second his body hit the sheets.

She caressed his cheeks, peering into his eyes as she half lay over his body. Concern and something more was in her hazel eyes. Thorn didn't have a name for that something—he'd never seen it. But he imagined that's what love looked like.

"You did it." She bit her lip, her pretty eyes misting with tears. "You let yourself go for us."

Cam climbed on the bed, lying over the other half of his body. And he wasn't weirded out. It was…comforting, the other warm, solid body. When the other man wrapped a hand around his shoulder and worked his hand up to his neck, Thorn shuddered and shut his eyes. It was so fucking intimate.

He was being both invaded and eased at once, and it was too much.

"You did good," Cam murmured.

There was happiness in his voice. And pride. That got to Thorn. When the hell had anyone been proud of him? Anyone at all?

Tears hit the back of his eyes like a thousand electric-charged needles. The second he felt the waterworks coming, he bucked and tried to sit up, tried to escape. Together, they held him down.

"Don't go," Brenna whispered, brushing soft kisses over his mouth.

"We're here for you." Cam squeezed his shoulder. "Always will be."

And he lost it.

A hot well of tears sprang up, flowed over. His body was a flood of agony, release, need, fear, love. So fucking confusing and painful as sobs racked him. And they grew worse when Brenna and Cam wouldn't let him cover his face or roll over to hide his face in the sheets. They just watched and petted him like a wounded animal.

Their kindness and caring was everything he remembered wishing for when he'd been a boy wondering who his mother was and why she'd abandoned him to a father dealing drugs five feet from his bedroom in a rundown trailer. Everything he'd prayed for when money was low and drugs had grown scarce and his father had elected to take his frustration out on his younger son because the older was too big to beat. Thorn remembered eating flour and stealing canned food from the local minimart just to take the edge off the hunger gnawing his preadolescent belly.

When the tears subsided, his eyes stung, his nose ran. Logic told him he should be incredibly embarrassed. How fucking unmanly, to cry after an orgasm. Instead, he didn't think he'd ever felt more released. Unburdened.

Clean and ready to make a new start.

Chapter Ten

🔊

"Tell me about it," Brenna asked, wiping away his tears with gentle fingers as noonday sunlight poured through the bedroom windows. "Please."

Thorn sucked in a deep breath and glanced at Cam. The same request lurked there.

"You two are like a heavyweight champ with a mean one-two punch. It was just...really intense." He sniffled and hoped it looked manly somehow. "I've never been that blown away."

"We wanted to do that for you." She kissed him again. "We wanted you to just *be* with us."

"But the real you," Cam added. "Not who you are with every other woman you take to bed. We want to make sure you understand this isn't just a fifteen-minute fuck."

Oh, he got the message. "Mission accomplished—and with all the subtlety of a steamroller."

Brenna and Cam shared a quick glance and a smile, then beamed it at him, and he felt like a part of the inner circle. Yeah, they'd taken from him, but they'd also given back a gentle understanding he'd never had in his life. They surrounded him with it, and if he believed in such New Age crap, he'd say he felt like he was glowing with it.

He swallowed. "I was just...not sure about letting go. It hasn't worked out so well for me in the past."

"What sort of past?" Cam demanded.

"Oh, the usual. Shitty childhood that warped me. No mom. Dad was a drug addict and dealer, blah, blah, blah. I don't want to make excuses. It's just always been easier and safer not to give a shit about anything or anyone."

"You never get hurt that way," Brenna murmured.

Exactly. Thorn didn't say it. Why state the obvious? Because one look at Cam's face told him the detective understood.

"You know we're not accepting that."

"No shit." *But now what?* "But I should beat the hell out of you for making me look like a pussy."

"We weren't trying to make you look like a pussy," Cam placated. "Just human. Just you."

And that was the only thing keeping him from getting really pissed. They hadn't meant to tear him down and kick him. They meant to strip his defenses and get to know the real him.

Would they like him if they *really* knew him?

Thorn took a swipe at his heavy, itchy eyes. "Here I am. In all my fucking glory. Now what?"

Brenna looked at Cam, then shot him a coy smile. "Now, it's your turn. We're putting ourselves in your hands."

Quickly, Thorn got the picture. This was some sort of trust thing. Cam had started the ball rolling, and Brenna had picked it up and ran. They'd broken him down to prove they'd be there for him. Fuck if it hadn't worked too. He had no doubt either would be there if he needed them. Now they were showing they had trust in him by turning themselves over to him. Clever…

Now, he wanted to show them exactly what he could do.

"It isn't a power game," Cam warned.

Thorn scowled. Duh! He wasn't an idiot. "You want me to know the power exchange runs both ways."

"That's part of it."

"You want me to know you're both willing to be totally with me."

"You're getting closer. But it's also about the experience you'll have when you're not trying to protect yourself all the time."

"You think it will be better?"

"Wasn't it a few minutes ago?" Cam challenged. "Wasn't the orgasm stronger because you just let go and gave into the pleasure and emotion?"

Fucker had a point. He sighed. "Anything else?"

Cam clapped him on the shoulder. "You make the calls. We trust you."

God, he couldn't believe he was having this deep conversation with a naked man while stealing glances at a bare babe he couldn't wait to touch. Too strange... But if the last twelve hours had taught him anything, it was to just go with the flow.

Two days ago, if Thorn had heard those words from any sexual partner, that would have been an immediate green light to move in, mow down, and bolt. Now...he couldn't do that. He was invested in them. He cared if they hurt, if they didn't feel pleasure. The idea of a fuck and run disturbed him. Hell, if he pulled that crap here, what did he have to go back to or look forward to except more long nights with nameless whores? Or his own hand?

Thorn glanced around the room and spotted Cam's nightstand. He yanked it open and found exactly what he was looking for. He found square foil packets and tossed a handful in the middle of the bed.

Walking to Brenna, he took handfuls of her damp tresses in his fists and locked her hazel gaze into his. "You sure about this? I can be a real son of a bitch."

"You can also be very intense and caring. You and Cam make me feel safe and adored, and those are things I'd been looking for my whole life." She caressed his cheek. "I'm sure."

Couldn't argue with logic. "Lie on the bed, back flat. Fit the edge of the mattress under the crook of your knees."

Brenna leapt to do his bidding and quickly positioned herself on the bed, looking up at him with unblinking trust.

Totally amazing.

Thorn swallowed then turned to Cam. This was more difficult. He'd pictured—hoped—that someday he'd find a woman to care about, so Brenna barging into his heart made it easier to accept. Cameron...

"Man, I never saw this coming."

The detective shrugged. "Honestly, I didn't either."

"Are we doing more together than just sharing her?"

Thorn no more than said the words and Cam's cock jerked and stood up straight.

"I guess that gives me an answer," Thorn said wryly.

Cam grimaced then turned serious. "I think you know how I feel about it. But right now is all up to you."

"Whatever happens...happens?"

Dark hair brushed Cam's stout neck as he nodded.

Holy shit. "So if I wanted to fuck you...?"

"If that's what you need to feel close to us, that's the whole point."

No hesitation on Cam's part, just a blunt answer. Truth was, Thorn didn't really know what he needed. But he was going to start with what he was comfortable with and see where it headed.

"Lie down next to Brenna, flat on your back, a little higher up on the bed."

Cam did exactly as he requested, and the sight of them there, naked and waiting just for him, made his dick stand up and want to tango again.

"Scoot over a little bit." Thorn patted Brenna's hip, and she nudged, making room between her and Cam.

Easing down on the bed between them, he turned to Brenna and laid his mouth over hers, gliding a hand over her breast and its stiff nipple. Easing his hand a bit lower, he realized that she was soaking wet.

"Did sucking me off with Cam's hand to help you turn you on?"

"Yes," she whimpered.

"I love you wet, baby."

"It's a constant state around you two."

Thorn smiled, feeling incredibly at ease, even when he turned this gaze to Cam. He was about to cross all kinds of personal lines here, and at the moment, he was nothing more than aroused and happy. Weird, but he wasn't going to examine it now.

He sat up between them, his left hand still toying with Brenna's pussy, honing in on her clit. Cam was watching. Every move. Nothing got past the detective.

But when Thorn reached out and grabbed Cam's cock. His dark, muscled body tensed, bowed. He lifted his hips and grabbed handfuls of the blankets in his big fists.

Sweet. He liked the power he had over them both, no denying that. But he also reveled in the fact he was giving them both pleasure. Now to turn up the heat.

With one hand, he worked Brenna's clit, the other stroked Cam's cock. Their mewls and groans made his blood burn. Her breath hitched and her fair skin flushed pretty, telling him she was well on her way to orgasm. Cam's whole body tightened, and in Thorn's hand, the man's dick swelled to beyond-impressive lengths. Staying focused wasn't easy, and he had to. The more they responded, the more he wanted to give them.

The more he refused to give up until he gave them the sort of pleasure they had given him.

Thorn slung an arm around Brenna's waist and pulled her closer. When she was nearly under him, he broke away from them long enough to don a condom. As soon as it was rolled on, he eased on top of her, latched onto her nipple and slid deep inside her. She took him in a single thrust.

As he reached the hilt, she gasped and reached out for

Cam beside her. She threaded her fingers through his, grabbing his hand for support.

Thorn reinstated his grip on Cam's cock and, elbow braced on the bed, he stroked Cam from root to tip. He repeated the process again and again and again, sinking into the heaven of Brenna's body and letting the hot clasp of her pussy surround him, all while stroking Cam in a slow tease. Holding the other man in his hand was shockingly erotic. He could feel the blood pump through Cam's cock, feel every twitch and jump and engorged vein under that satin skin.

The detective's lips parted and he groaned, pulsed under his fingers. Close, but not yet.

Easing off Cam, he turned his focus for the moment to Brenna, pounding her with hard strokes, fitting one hand under her to tilt her hips up just right.

"Get your hand on her clit."

Cam hurried to comply.

Thorn fucked her—hard. Every thrust shook the bed but he kept her tight under him. He could feel Cam's fingers now and again brushing the base of his cock as the detective worked over her slippery clit. Her skin turned damp, her breathing gasping and sporadic. She clutched at Thorn's hair, and he sank down into the sensation of a little pain with a whole lot of pleasure. Her pussy was one sultry, juicy place to be as she tightened and tightened all around him.

"Close," Cam told him.

"Oh yeah," he could feel it.

Her exhalations became farther apart and louder. Against Thorn's chest, her nipples stabbed him. He clutched her, loving everything about the way she felt around him, the moonlight and floral smell of her, the way she clung to him as if nothing else mattered.

And then she shattered, crying out so loud he wondered if Cam's neighbors would call 911. Her body shook, shuddered. If she'd had an orgasm problem previously—issue solved. Totally. The woman threw her body into pleasure now, and it showed. He grimaced, barely holding onto his own release. How easy it would be to just let go... But a glance at Cam reminded him that he wasn't done yet.

Soon, he slowed, pushing in as if gently easing through honey. Then back out in a wicked slow pace. A few minutes of that, and she went from sated to gasping at the friction-tingling sensation all over again. Thorn knew by the way she tensed, frowned, bit her lip and moaned.

Withdrawing from her body, Thorn stood up and over them. "You really trust me?"

Brenna didn't even hesitate. "Yes."

Thorn turned his stare in Cam's direction. "You?"

"Yes. Like I said, this is your show."

With a long, low shudder of breath, Thorn tore off his condom and plunged back into Brenna. He gritted his teeth against the instant jolt of pleasure. Riding her bareback was stunning. He hadn't done that to any female since he was a teenager, but holy fucking wow!

He managed to croak out, "I'm clean."

"I'm not on the Pill," she said, her voice shaking in subtle warning.

He soothed a honey-brown curl away from her cheek. "I'll be careful."

A stroke, another. Damn, it was like heaven. Someday, he'd love the chance to sink deep without a condom, know it was okay to bathe her womb with seed...and watch Cam do the same. He didn't know where the hell this thought was going, but he knew that Brenna being pregnant by one of them would arouse him out of his fucking mind. Even the thought was putting him on edge.

Carefully, he withdrew then turned to Cam. "You want a taste of her pussy?"

He nodded.

Thorn grabbed the base of his cock. "It's right here."

Their eyes met, Cam's dark gaze did not express revulsion or fear but arousal and reassurance. *Are you sure?* he asked silently.

"Suck me," he whispered.

A corner of Cam's mouth lifted. "This will be new for me, so if I'm not great at it, you'll forgive me."

Thorn snorted. "You'll get practice."

Cam didn't refute him but instead sat up on the bed. Thorn stood over it, and Cam grabbed him by the hips. Thorn closed his eyes and lost himself in the electric anticipation.

He didn't have to wait long. Wet, hot, and with all the suction of a Hoover, Cam's mouth dazzled. His tongue was in motion, on a mission, laving the head of Thorn's cock, rubbing the sides, cradling his length. Without thought, Thorn sank his fingers into Cam's hair, arched his back and began to fuck the man's mouth. For a reported amateur, he gave some of the best head Thorn had ever had. Damn.

Beside them, Brenna watched, wide-eyed.

"This okay with you, baby?" Thorn managed to get out. Though if she wasn't okay, he wasn't sure he could stop at this point.

"It's amazing to watch." Her voice trembled as her nipples went totally erect. "You look so...aroused. Both of you."

With a whole new and mind-boggling intensity, yes. Despite having two orgasms already today and a handful last night, his body was already racing for the finish line again, and the sight of Cam's mouth stretched wide over his dick, the man's strong fingers gouging into his hips, was bringing his need to the fore faster than warp speed.

Fuck. This wasn't about him. He needed to be focused on really being himself with them, on breaking down their barriers so they were totally themselves with him. He didn't want to be the only one with a naked soul here. He also wanted to feel exactly who they were with all their defenses gone.

Boy, wasn't that new for him?

Hugging Cam against him, Thorn leaned in and said, "You're too fucking good at that. You're about to undo me."

Then he eased away. Cam turned a smug grin up at him with a red, swollen mouth that Thorn found even more arousing. Hell, had he turned gay?

One glance in Brenna's direction, at her erect nipples and slick pussy she now idly touched, and he knew better. He'd kill to be inside her again. And he would — soon, but now…he had other business.

Thorn leaned between them and reached to the center of the bed, then tossed the detective a condom.

"Here. Get this on."

Cam blinked, staring at the little foil square. "Because?"

"I'm in charge. Put it on and stand up."

With a groan and a very hard dick, Cam did as Thorn said. But his body language screamed for release, taut shoulders, dick hugging his flat belly looking angry and red as he covered it with the condom.

Thorn reached over to Brenna, caressed her hair, then let his touch drift down her body, over her breasts, to her swollen pussy. "You ready for more, baby?"

She whimpered when his fingers grazed her clit. "Please."

With a firm grip, he grabbed her hips and dragged them to the edge of the bed, her legs dangling over. Then he backed away.

"I'm gloved up," Cam announced, hands on his lean hips, cock standing straight up. "I assume I'm giving rather than receiving?"

Like the whole thought of being penetrated didn't faze Cam in the least. Thorn had to admit the guy impressed the hell out of him — and aroused him.

"Yes...for now." He stepped to the side, away from Brenna's open body. "Fuck her."

Cam smiled his approval, approached Brenna and sank deep in one ruthless thrust. She gasped at the invasion and wrapped her pale, firm legs around his bronzed back. They looked hot together. Amazing. He'd love to just stand and watch them. Cam knew exactly how to please a woman, tilting her hips, fucking her with slow, relentless thrusts, murmuring his desire and pleasure in her ear. But he could also see that Brenna was special to Cam. The way he covered her body protectively, the rapturous look on his face, the adoring caresses, they all told Thorn that Brenna wasn't just any woman to the detective. Which suited him. She wasn't just any woman to Thorn, either.

Not taking his eyes off the couple, he backed into the bedroom, grabbed a little bottle he'd seen earlier, then sauntered back in. Time to liven up this party. And if his hands shook and his belly flip-flopped...he'd survive. Somehow, this was right. His gut told him that.

Donning another condom, he made use of the bottle but kept it gripped it in his hands. Then he approached the other two.

Already, Brenna's erratic breathing told him orgasm was near. And Cam... Every muscle of his wide back bunched with effort, every drive into her body ended with a tight clench of his ass, a groan torn from his chest. Sweat slicked his skin as he gripped her tighter, thrust deeper.

Bending over Cam's back, Thorn murmured in his ear, "Stop."

The man's entire body tensed as he buried himself deep in Brenna's body and held her in an unyielding grip. "Fuck!"

"Soon," Thorn promised with a chuckle. "Now it's time for you to receive."

Cam stilled. "Seriously?"

"While you keep giving it to Brenna. You got a problem

with that?"

The pause was long and chafed against Thorn. Coming to this decision hadn't been easy for him, but his instinct told him that if he wanted to hold this together and have anything lasting with these two, he was going to have to open his boundaries. Cam had been pushing him since this started. Now he was going to back out?

Cam turned and stared at him over his shoulder. Just a glance from those dark eyes, and Thorn saw the man's mingled anticipation and fear. "Go easy on me. I've never...received."

So the guy in college had never penetrated Cam. Somehow, it seemed fitting to Thorn that he be Cam's first. He cared about the guy...who was about to become way more than a friend. He adored Brenna. Why not admit it? Getting deep inside her blew him away every time. Would being inside Cam be as mind-blowing?

Thorn dumped a little more oil from the bottle in his hands and set it on the nightstand. He worked it over Cameron's back entrance with his fingertips before inserting a finger which slid in easily—and revealed a tight passage that would be a sexual pressure cooker for his dick. Sweating at the thought, he twisted in a second finger and eased them apart. Cam tensed, then settled back.

Leaning around Cam's broad back, Thorn looked at Brenna. "He still hard?"

She wiggled her hips and nodded enthusiastically. "Yes, and it's killing me. Hurry!"

Right, like he wanted to rush through his chance to strip Saint Cam bare. Like he wanted to inhale the experience of really being with the two of them. No way, no how, not when he'd waited his whole life.

Slowly, he added a third finger to Cam's rear. This time, the detective hissed. His shoulders stiffened.

"Hurt?" Thorn asked.

Cam grunted. "You got more in mind than running your mouth and a little finger play?"

The man was asking for it. Honest to goodness asking for it. Thorn figured he'd better give it to him.

Withdrawing his fingers, Thorn took his cock in hand and fitted the head against Cam's tight entrance. His hands shook, his belly took a nosedive, his balls were on fire.

If this went off as he expected it to, he supposed that someday Cam would be his first. He shivered at the thought and wondered if taking someone inside him who mattered would be as shattering as getting inside someone he cared about. Probably. Meaningful sex, now that he was having it for the first time in his life, was just way fucking better than an anonymous screw.

"Yeah, I got more in mind. This will be totally easy, man," Thorn promised Cam. "Smooth as glass."

After a brief hesitation, Cam nodded. "Do it. I want you to."

Caressing Cam's taut cheeks, Thorn spread him and assumed a wide stance as he eased inside, nudging gently. Cam gasped. Thank God the bed was waist high. Thorn wrapped his arm around the man's waist. Under his hand, he could feel the detective's abdominal muscles tense and ripple.

"Fuck!" Cam muttered.

"Not quite..." Thorn gritted out as the tight ring of muscle stopped him. He pushed harder, banging against it a few times until it gave way and he sank deep, deep.

Oh, shit! Tight and hot, Cam's ass had a grip on his dick guaranteed to rip away his self-control in about two-point-two seconds. The hard swell of Cam's prostate dragged over the most sensitive places. How the fuck was he supposed to last through this?

Gingerly, he withdrew, then eased in again. His assessment didn't change. If anything, his brain just fried more. And Cam, so responsive, tensed underneath him, moaning, hips bobbing. Brenna gasped, and Thorn smiled. Nice to know his impromptu plan was likely to work.

Sliding in to the hilt again, Thorn leaned over Cam, plastering his chest to the man's back. He slid the silky dark hair away from his ear and murmured, "Ready to fuck?"

Cam shuddered, and Thorn saw his eyes close. "Yeah."

Thorn reached down to Brenna, petted her shoulder, cupped her breast. "You?"

She whimpered and nodded frantically.

"Good. I'm driving the bus, kids. Hang on for the ride."

With that, Thorn eased back, nearly to the head, before shoving back inside Cam again. His thrust pushed the detective into Brenna, who gasped and dug her nails into Cam's shoulders. God, it was good. Mind-bogglingly good. Beyond-known-language good. This was going to be a fast and furious ride. No way to prolong something this sensational.

Better to just enjoy while it lasted.

Pulling back again, Thorn thrust hard, deep, again and again. Without pause. Without mercy. He filled his hands with Cam's hips, sweat breaking out across his body. Around him, Cam tightened, his body tensed. As his pulse jumped, Thorn could feel it in the sheath of the body around him, beating at his dick, his self-control. Under Cam, Brenna was groaning, flushing, as every demanding entry bled into the next in a furious rhythm that left everyone breathless.

Cam lowered his head to Brenna and devoured her mouth. Brenna's hands sank into Cam's hair, and he could see the desperation in her touch. It was more arousing than he'd imagined. The whole scene was. Damn, he was about to lose it—and refused to do it before the others.

Shifting his hips, Thorn changed his angle, focusing on the little bead of Cam's prostate. The detective's head rolled back on his neck. His shoulders strained. He let out a growl and his hands latched onto Brenna like a life raft in a raging current.

Thank God, because Thorn could feel the heat rising like flares off the sun's surface. Desire brewed and bubbled in his belly, in his balls. The need to come was a hot pressure, gripping him tighter and tighter. Sweat trickled down his face, between his shoulder blades.

If he didn't act fast, he was going to lose it first.

Reaching under Cam, Thorn found Brenna's clit. Slick, swollen, begging—and if her gasp was anything to go by— very sensitive.

He rubbed her, the friction of his fingers over the bundle of nerves designed for maximum impact. Not too hard or too soft, but enough to drive her past the point of no return.

Brenna began to moan and thrash, her head swinging from side to side as she grew more urgent, her body tensing, clasping, ready...

"Oh...oh, shit," Cam groaned. "Fuck!"

Brenna let out a long wail, the echo of her cry of ecstasy bouncing off the walls. Like a house of cards, Cam tensed next, his passage tightening and fluttering around Thorn's cock as the man let out labored breath after labored breath.

Then Cam's entire body seized up and released with a long cry that mingled with Brenna's. Part plea, part benediction, the sound, coupled with the thunder of his own blood in his ears, crushed the last of Thorn's resistance. The grasping clasp of Cam's body on him was tight and unavoidable and one of the most amazing things he'd ever felt in his life.

Locked him deep inside Cam, need boiled up inside Thorn and spilled over in a scalding rush of sensation. With a throaty cry, the gush of pleasure flamed inside him, so unique and amazing, Thorn swore he'd never felt anything quite like it. Being with the two of them—in every way—was simply life-altering.

But neither of them moved, said a word. What if they didn't feel the same?

Chapter Eleven

ᔥ

After showers all around, Brenna wandered into the kitchen in one of Cam's oversized t-shirts which hung to her knees. She watched Thorn prowl through the refrigerator. Cam approached her from behind and dropped a kiss on her shoulder, then peeked around her to look at the available chow too.

Watching them, she bit her lip. When had they both become so dear to her? Who would have ever imagined that she'd come to love men who broke into her house in the middle of the night and used her pleasure against her to find her father?

With just a handful of days left until her father's trial, she had to wonder what would happen after that. The sex between the three of them was so intense...felt so important not just to her body but her heart. When she saw the looks on their faces deep in the midst of pleasure, she could swear they felt the same. But now? They stared into the refrigerator as if nothing was more important than an afternoon snack.

Maybe she should just feed them, then ask where the hell this unusual relationship was going. They might not care that she loved them, Cam for his sharp yet sensitive side, Thorn for the gruff front that hid a wealth of goodness in his heart. But if she told them how she felt and they rejected her, at least she'd know. Better than leaving, wondering if things would have ended differently if she'd just spoken up.

"Oh, let me." Brenna shouldered her way past them and grabbed some chicken breasts out of the refrigerator. Sour cream and milk came next, then fresh broccoli and mushrooms. She deposited all that near the stove, grabbed a few spices and some pasta from the pantry. She could make *something* out of this.

"What—?"

Brenna held up a hand to stave Cam's question off. "You want to eat, let me do my thing."

"Let me help you. I can cook."

"I can cook better and faster all by myself."

As she clattered around the kitchen and took out a pan and a bowl, the doorbell rang.

Everyone in the kitchen froze, then Cam darted into action, running for the door. Everyone followed. Brenna hadn't noticed weapons on them earlier, but both men drew their guns.

Cam looked through the peephole. "Shit."

Before she could question him, he threw the door wide open. In the October chill, a lone man in black stood there, looking nervously over her shoulder.

"Curtis?" she choked.

He nodded and charged into the house, slamming the door and locking it behind him. He reached for her, one hand digging around her arm.

Thorn pulled him away with a growl. "You want to keep your balls attached to your body, you don't grab her."

"She's my daughter."

"Who you've never been much of a father to," Cam pointed out. "Why are you here?"

Curtis' shrewd gaze darted between the two half-dressed men and her clad only in a man's shirt and drew some accurate conclusions. Surprise skittered across his face. But he also looked dirty and tired and hungry. Strained. Whatever he'd been about to say regarding the choices in her love life, he swallowed.

"I got your message. Someone came for you?"

"How did you get my address?" Cam demanded.

"Got a buddy of mine to run your license plate."

Cameron swore and shook his head.

Curtis couldn't have cared less. "Tell me, someone came looking for you? Who?"

Thorn let Curtis go, but placed his body between hers and her father's. Brenna tried not to be touched but that was impossible. He really was so protective and caring in his growly way.

"Yeah, asshole," Thorn answered. "They did. Two goons tried to abduct her at your little mountain love shack. You know, the one where you keep the girlfriends her age you like to inflict pain on."

Curtis had the good grace to wince. "I didn't think Julio knew about the place. I thought she'd be safe there until after the trial."

"Oh, come on. Julio makes it his business to know everything about everyone involved with him. I wouldn't be surprised if they knew she was your daughter."

At that suggestion, Curtis turned white. "I'm sorry. Really sorry."

"You've been a fuckup her whole life," Thorn accused.

"I know."

"And nothing has changed." Brenna frowned, confusion and pain sliding through her. "I came to Arizona to talk to you about why you just left me."

"Look, now isn't the best time…"

"It never is!"

Curtis raked a pale hand through short, graying hair. "I knew your aunt and her husband would raise you better than I could. Hell, when you were born, I was already ass deep in trouble. I've been in prison twice since you were a toddler. You didn't know that, did you? Your aunt kept it from you. Honey, I'm just bad. I don't know any other way of life now. If

I hadn't given you up, you would have gone into foster care, and God knows what would have happened to you then. I cared for you the best way I knew how."

Which wasn't much. Curtis had always been about Curtis, and that would never change. "You forgot most every birthday."

"I thought of you every July seventh of every year."

So he did know her birthday? "And every Christmas except the last one."

"Who do you think sent your aunt that Santa Claus money when you were a kid? I know it doesn't make up for my absence—"

"It doesn't."

"And maybe we're just broken. Maybe it will never be repaired. I didn't know how to be a father or how to care until you were too old for me to just waltz back into your life. I'm sorry. It's in the past, and I can't fix it. Right now, I just want to keep you alive." He turned to Cam, glanced at Thorn. "I'm being followed."

"Marco's men?"

"I'm sure of it. The Feds are easy to spot. They stick out like stink on shit wherever I go."

"Why trust us?" Cam asked.

"I can tell by the way you're treating Brenna that you're not going to do anything that would hurt her. She may be pissed at me, but throwing me to Marco's wolves would devastate her."

It was true. Brenna didn't bother to refute him.

Cam leaned in. "I would have protected you from the start if you'd let me."

Curtis rolled his eyes. "You don't get it. Marco has eyes, ears and guns everywhere. You're crazy, Detective, if you think that you and a few uniforms could keep him from offing me. Marco's men got close to me when I was hiding. I overheard them say they knew Brenna was here and they were going to nab her and use her to bring me out of hiding. I had to head them off. We've got to get out of here now."

With a curse, Cam reached for his cell phone. "Let me get backup."

Thorn glanced out the window. "Too late."

Gun drawn, Cam charged toward the back door and lifted the blinds a fraction. And swore.

"They're here?" Her voice shook, every bit as much as her insides.

Cam nodded grimly and punched a few buttons on his cell phone. In less than ten words, he'd managed to call for help.

There was going to be shooting, blood and death. She could feel it. Brenna tried not to panic, but what did a waitress with a few college credits from the lazy city of Muenster, Texas know about gun battles? Nothing at all.

"Brenna is most important. We get her out safely, no matter what," Cam said.

"Absolutely," Thorn said.

Her father nodded in agreement.

The detective groped around on a nearby counter and found his car keys, then tossed them to Thorn. "Get her in the car and get ready. We're going to lure them into the house. When we do, get the hell out of here. Hide her on the floorboards. Don't let them take cheap shots at her though the windows."

Thorn looked like he wanted to argue, but one look at Brenna's face and he swallowed it. "We'll go. How soon before your boys arrive, Cam?"

"Less than five."

With a grim nod, Thorn took her by the hand and clapped Cam on the shoulder. "Call us when it's over."

Tears welled in Brenna's eyes. They couldn't just leave

Cam to a fairly certain death. "I won't go."

"Please." Cam stroked her cheek. "Please. It would kill me if you were hurt. I love you."

She gasped. Really? Truly? "I love you too. I would die if something happened—"

He pressed a quick kiss to her lips, stopping her words. "Shh. Go with Thorn. He'll keep you safe. I do this all the time. I'll be fine."

Thorn stepped up to Cam. "Man, I—"

"Later. We'll hash it out later."

If there was a later.

Thorn sighed. "You always were a heroic son of a bitch. You're the best friend I've got."

Surprise rolled through Cam's dark eyes. "I'm more than that."

Thorn didn't look away or flinch from the truth. "Yeah."

Cam shoved them toward the garage door. "Go."

Thorn dragged Brenna away—only to be stopped by Curtis' embrace.

"Take care, little girl."

Brenna paused. She'd spent years—decades—infuriated with this man who'd stayed around only long enough to sire her and drop her on her aunt's doorstep. At times she'd wondered if she hated him. She'd rehearsed speeches through the years designed to tell him with razor perfection how much she loathed him and had no respect for his behavior.

But in what could be the last moments for any or all of them, the speeches and hatred flew out of her head. "You came back to make sure I was okay."

That fact astounded her. Somewhere, somehow, in his way, he actually cared.

He nodded, looking every one of his fifty-six years. "I don't want you to pay for my sins."

"Company is closing in fast, boys and girls," Thorn growled as he stared out the window through the crack between the curtains. "Let's go."

The bounty hunter jerked on her arm and led her out of the kitchen, toward the garage. Heart pumping, hurting, she looked back to find Cam handing her father a weapon and loading another."

God, please let them be okay.

They didn't make it to the garage door before two hired guns crashed through Cam's back window in a hail of shattered glass. They landed on their feet, and one kicked out, knocking the gun from her father's hand.

Thorn shoved her behind him and around a corner, into the laundry room between the kitchen and the garage, with a terrible curse. "Stay."

Their eyes met, and his told her that he'd defend her to the death. Solemn. Heavy. Concerned.

Then he was gone, still blocking the doorway but edging closer to Cameron.

"Curtis," one of them said in mock friendliness as he straightened his shades. "You've been hard to find. Mr. Marco would like a few words with you."

No doubt, he was one cold dude. An assassin who would think nothing of pulling the trigger. Brenna could tell just by looking at his craggy face and piercing eyes. Peering between the crack in the door, she saw her father shudder in fear.

"MacIntyre," her father began. "I—"

"You got no excuses. Come with us quietly."

"You're not taking my witness," Cam vowed.

He and Thorn both eased near her father, weapons drawn. They looked big and fearless and invincible, but she knew one bullet could change everything.

Marco's goon gave her lovers a quick once over. "Put your weapons down."

"Fuck off," Thorn spat.

She saw the hired gun look in her direction.

And felt the barrel of a gun against the back of her head a moment later.

Cold fear gripped her as a rough hand dragged her to her feet and shoved her into the kitchen.

"Let's try this again. Put your weapons down now or your mutual girlfriend will be missing the back half of her skull in two seconds."

Cam cursed and dropped his to the hardwood floor.

Thorn gritted his teeth, and a thousand regrets seemed to cross his face before he did the same.

"Splendid. The three of you gave a great peep show through the bedroom window."

Brenna could just hear the smarmy tone, and it made her want to claw his eyes out.

"Let her go, Marco," Cam said through gritted teeth. "She's got nothing to do with this."

Marco? As in Julio Marco? Brenna risked a glance over her shoulder to find one mean asshole, complete with soulless dark eyes and a scar from temple to jaw. His crooked nose and pierced lip didn't give her the warm fuzzies either.

Marco looked at Cam like he was an insect. "Don't be stupid, Martinez. And no more of your standard lines or I'll just shoot her for the pleasure of crushing you."

Brenna gasped as his words injected cold fear into her bloodstream. He'd do it. That whip-sharp voice told her so.

"Curtis," Marco continued, "Are you willing to come with us now or do we need to demonstrate on your daughter what we'll do to you if you fail to cooperate?"

"I'll go."

"No!" Brenna gasped. If he stayed, maybe they had a chance. Backup was on the way. As long as he was here, there was hope. If Curtis left…she knew she'd never see him again.

"He'll kill you."

Curtis sent her a gaze filled with regret, his hazel eyes so like her own. "Better me than you."

A moment later, a shot rang out. Brenna barely heard a whistle of a sound when one of Marco's assassins not two feet from her fell to the ground, a bloom of blood spreading across his chest. Police backup!

Marco and the other goon searched frantically for the source of the shots. They'd come through the smashed-in back window, but from trees? Bushes? She didn't know. And Marco didn't seem inclined to stay and find out.

"We've got to get the fuck out of here!" Marco hollered.

He kept his gun trained on her and placed her directly in front of him, like a human shield. The other assassin, MacIntyre, ducked behind the kitchen island.

"Don't move," Marco said to Thorn and Cam. "Or your girlfriend gets it."

They both froze and sent her stares that reached out to embrace her they way they clearly wanted to with their arms. They loved her. Cam had said it. Thorn hadn't, but his face shouted that fact now.

It gave her hope, strength. They'd endure whatever. Somehow.

"Come here," Marco said to her father.

Curtis looked scared out of his mind as he put one foot in front of the other, toward her and the criminal.

Brenna saw Thorn cut a glance to Cam, who gave a barely perceptible nod. They were planning something. No. Oh, God. She didn't want to die, but the thought of them being hurt...it was like ripping her apart from the inside out. Marco and his men hadn't come here for her. She didn't believe they really wanted to kill her. They wouldn't hesitate if they had to, but she hoped that by stalling, it would give Cam's peers enough time to figure this out. If Cam and Thorn jumped in...

NO! she mouthed to them. Neither was paying attention.

Chapter Twelve

ൠ

As one, Thorn leapt on Marco, slamming him back against the oven. Cam dove to the ground, grabbed his gun and popped off a shot, hitting Marco in the thigh. He grunted and cursed in her ear but his hold on her dissolved.

Cam grabbed her arm and threw her out of the fray, next to Curtis, who fumbled a gun in his shaking hands.

Marco's henchman gave Cam a mighty shove. He fell back against the island, his back slamming into the counter. Thorn shot MacIntyre in the next moment, and turned to Marco, who already had his gun raised to Cameron, aiming right for his head. Brenna could hear a silent ticktock of milliseconds in her head. It was now...or bye-bye Cameron. She pushed him to the ground.

Which left the gun pointing directly at her.

Marco's hand tightened on the weapon, and he shot her a cold smile. Shit, he was going to pull the trigger. It was there in his empty eyes.

With a roar, Curtis leapt to put his body between her and Marco. She screamed as Cam launched himself at Marco, whose body slammed back against the oven again.

Despite that, he still managed to squeeze the trigger.

A moment later, Brenna fell to the floor under her father's weight. Her head hit the kitchen island, and pain exploded at the back of her skull. She closed her eyes against the rush of agony.

Pounding footsteps made her open them again. Marco turned to run, hobbling due to his gunshot wound, but he still made it to the front door. Cam gave chase.

"Stop, asshole!"

Marco just kept running, right past large bushes on either side of the door. As soon as Marco ran past them, a pair of cops concealed in those bushes jumped the criminal from behind, disarmed him with a knee in his back and a fist in his hair. They read him his rights.

Brenna groaned, trembled and turned to her father, to thank him for saving her.

He lay on top of her in a heap, motionless. There was a little red hole right between his wide open eyes.

She screamed and scrambled back in utter shock. He slithered off her, still.

Brenna had come to Arizona for closure with her relationship with her father, but not like this. When she'd boarded the plane, she'd never imagined it would end in his death.

Suddenly, Thorn was there, raising her to her feet, curling her body into his, turning her gaze into his shoulder and away from Curtis' sightless eyes.

"I'm sorry, baby. So sorry."

Dead, dead, dead... The word was a chant in her brain. And she knew it would hit her at some point that he father was no more. But right now, shock and a gladness that Thorn and Cam were both okay filled her.

She couldn't feel her legs. Dizziness assailed her. Her head throbbed mercilessly. The edges of her vision started to close in. Then...nothing.

* * * * *

Brenna awoke to sterile smells that assaulted her nostrils. She hadn't died, right? Death couldn't smell this chemically clean...

Her head ached as if someone had been using it as a drum at a heavy metal concert. She was lying on something soft. But she was definitely alive. Thanks to Curtis.

Memories assaulted her—good and bad. Julio Marco arrested...her father dead. It saddened her that they'd never had a real father-daughter relationship. But he'd made choices—to be a criminal, to get involved with Marco, to jump in front of the bullet. He'd cared enough about her to give his life so that she could live. That in itself confirmed that, in his way, he'd cared.

A moment later, the sensation that someone was staring besieged her.

Gingerly, she opened her eyes to a semidark room, thank God. Moonlight poured in through a little window. The ceiling was sterile white.

But the two concerned faces above her made her heart lurch with relief.

"You're here..."

Cameron grabbed her hand. "We wouldn't be anywhere else."

Thorn caressed her cheek. "We haven't left your side for the last four hours, despite some pissed-off cops."

Brenna lifted her head a fraction and glanced past them to see two uniforms guarding the door, wearing identical glowers.

"They have questions."

"Yes, but we didn't want you to wake up alone." Cameron kissed her cheek.

Thorn brushed his mouth over her lips softly. "You'll be okay if we answer the police now?"

She nodded.

"The doctor wants to see you anyway," Cam noted then backed away from the bed. "I'm sorry about your father."

"Me too," Thorn nodded. "I didn't love the guy, but..."

"I know. You tried. I thank you for it." She squeezed his hand.

A brisk forty-something woman in a white coat came in and shooed her men away. She did a quick exam, and asked a few questions before giving her a clean bill of health.

She rose from the bed gingerly. Two seconds after donning her clothes, the uniformed officers descended on her, asking a bevy of questions. But it didn't take long. Evidently, her story corroborated Cam and Thorn's. Marco and his surviving goon were behind bars. Between Marco and his lackey, along with the sworn statements her father had already given, the police had managed to conduct a raid of Marco's secret properties and discovered dozens of illegal immigrants working against their will.

When Cam and Thorn returned to her draped-off corner of the emergency room to help her gather her things, they assured her that Marco would be going away to the big house for a long time.

It wouldn't save her father. He was gone, and she hoped that he could find the peace in death that he'd never found in life. She might never know what demons drove him to badness, but she understood now that he could never be hurt again and that he hadn't rejected her as much as he'd tried to protect her from the black life he'd built.

"What about your house?" Brenna asked Cam. "Marco and his guys trashed it."

"My buddies already did the cleanup on aisle five. New glass will be delivered tomorrow. Why don't you come see for yourself?"

Brenna cocked her head at his eager yet anxious expression. Did he fear she'd say no?

"I'd love to."

Cam brushed his lips over hers. "Good, as long as you're there, maybe I could persuade you to stay a while."

She tamped down an excited smile. "How long is a while?"

He shrugged. "Fifty years. To start."

Casting her shocked glance Thorn's way, he looked tense too. Did he also want her to stay and was worried she wouldn't? What was up with these two?

"What about him?"

"I'm in," Thorn replied. "We've discussed it."

"So you've mapped out my whole future?"

Put that way, they both had the grace to look sheepish.

"Well," Cam began, "we had a thought. But we'd love to hear yours."

"Okay. Why don't I come stay for a few weeks with you two, and we'll see how it goes."

Thorn gritted his teeth and cursed. "That plan sucks."

Brenna sashayed closer to them, stopping between them to glance at one, then the other. Talk about unexpected… "What exactly did you have in mind?"

"A hell of a lot more than a vacation fling," Thorn groused. "We want you to move here. We want to make things permanent. I love you. God, I've never said that to anyone in my life," Thorn said in one breath. "Scarier than shit. But it's true. I care about you both. I've never had a personal life that meant more than a cheap fuck. You and Cam mean…everything."

Thorn wasn't great with words but sincerity ruled his face. It was impossible not to believe him.

Impossible not to be celebrating inside.

"Let me hear this plan you two cooked up."

Thorn opened his mouth but Cam cut him off. "We thought maybe you could move in with me. Us. Thorn will give up his trailer."

"Lars can have the piece of shit."

Cam sent him a glare, then turned back to her with an expression so placating, it was comical. "Then we hoped you would marry me."

She blinked once. Twice. Marriage? She'd known them less than thirty-six hours.

Yet she didn't doubt the fact she loved them both. They loved her and each other. Conventional, no. But no one's business. If she was happy with them, to hell with everyone else's opinion.

"Why not Thorn?"

Thorn himself supplied the answer. "Cam has family that will give a shit. Plus, he has health insurance, so that when the babies are born—"

Cam punched him in the arm. "We agreed to ease her into that, you idiot."

"I didn't put it all in one sentence."

Shaking his head, Cam closed his eyes. "I meant that maybe we wouldn't bring up the babies for a few months."

"Fuck that. I want to get started now."

Brenna bit her lip, trying not to laugh. This had to be the most offbeat, comical proposal a woman had ever received.

"Who's fathering these babies?" she ventured.

They both hesitated. Cam looked at Thorn and vice versa. Then Cam replied, "It doesn't matter to us if it doesn't matter to you."

It didn't, but she was glad to hear them say it.

"I'm not a breeding machine, boys. This would have to be planned. I wanted to finish college in the next few years. I hate waitressing and I want to make something more of my life."

"Sure," Cam agreed.

"Totally," Thorn said. "Babies can wait a few years, I guess."

He actually looked disappointed. Who would have imagined that the man who'd first tied her to a bed and treated her like a one-time fling would want to tie himself to them in every way possible in just a few short hours? Miracles never ceased. And she knew that love was their most unexpected miracle.

"Good. Law school takes time."

"Law school?" they echoed.

She shrugged. "I figure we need to round this out. Cam can arrest them. Thorn can find them if they skip bail, and I can prosecute them once they're captured. Deal?"

"Absolutely," Cam murmured against her mouth as he planted a long, sweet kiss on her.

Thorn elbowed him out of the way and laid a powerful kiss full of demand on her lips a moment later. Cam sidled up to her, kissing her neck. Someone fondled her breast. A hand drifted down to her ass and dipped between her legs. She felt herself go moist...just as one of the hospital staff standing at the door cleared her throat.

They looked up to find the nurse wearing a slightly shocked expression. She had Brenna's discharge papers and post-visit instructions. Thorn took them, and the two men guided her out of the emergency room and into the cool October evening.

"So was that a yes? Are we taking you home with us?" Cam asked, his expression so hopeful, she couldn't keep him dangling any longer.

"Please..." Thorn cajoled like a six-year-old asking for a candy bar.

For Thorn to use *that* word, his feelings had to be serious.

She smiled and looped her arms around them both. "Yes."

"You'll marry me?" Cam asked.

"Yes."

"You'll move in with us and have babies?"

She smiled, wondering at Thorn's new fascination with kids. "Yes."

They whooped and hollered, exchanging high-fives.

Her voice cut through the middle of that. "With conditions."

They abruptly stopped. "Conditions?"

"One, we meet Cam's family before the wedding and tell them the truth. I'm not hiding our relationship. If some of the babies turn out blonde and blue-eyed, I don't want them to have any questions."

Cam let out a big sigh and pressed his lips together. Eventually, he nodded. "You're right. It will be tough for them at first, but it's better if they know."

"You can meet Lars if you want, but I doubt it will be a pleasure. He's a first-class bastard." Thorn shrugged.

"We'll be telling him too, just in case. Two, Cam and I will have a legal wedding at the JP or something small, but the big bash will be our own private ceremony with family and friends, joining the three of us. I'll be inviting my family too. We'll see if they come. If they don't... I don't need their approval to be happy."

They both nodded as they approached Cam's truck. He unlocked it and eased her inside. Thorn ran around to the other side and sandwiched her in between them on the bench seat.

"Three," she went on. "I need names. Full names. I can't be living with, marrying and having babies of men whose full names I don't know."

"Cameron Eduardo Hector Rafael Martinez." He grimaced. "I had lots of uncles to be named after."

"Oh my gosh. I'll try to remember all that. Thorn?"

Cam leaned over her as he started the truck. "Yeah, what does that R. A. stand for? You've always refused to say, and no one at the stations knows."

"I like it that way." He released a long-suffering sigh. "The only person who knows is Lars and that's because he was old enough to remember the day I was born. Don't think he didn't torment me with it all my life. You will too. Nope, I'm not saying."

Brenna crossed her arms over her chest. "That's one of my conditions. Take it or leave it."

"Aw, fuck."

Cam laughed long and loud. "Spill it, man. We'll keep your secret."

"It will be just between us," Brenna assured.

He hesitated, then closed his eyes in defeat. "You will never, ever call me by this name at any moment of any day. I don't care how annoyed, ecstatic or aroused you might be. This never crosses your lips."

Brenna made an X over her heart. "You have my word."

Thorn shook his head, golden hair brushing his shoulders. He'd always be a bit wild and hard to tame, but she knew he'd be hers and Cam's.

"Rikard Alviss. Don't you dare laugh."

She looked at Cam and could see that he, too, was suppressing the major urge to bust out. Somehow, she managed to keep it down. Probably had something to do with the blood she tasted in her mouth after biting the inside of her cheek.

When she'd finally composed a straight face, she turned to Thorn. "Thank you for sharing. I'll make sure you don't regret it."

His face softened. "Baby, I could never regret sharing anything with you."

"Me, either," Cam confirmed. "I've never been happier."

Neither had she.

With a smile, she reached out and put a hand on each of their crotches. In seconds, she had a pair of erections beneath tight denim right at her fingertips.

"Care to go home and share more, then?"

Cameron peeled out of the parking lot while Thorn

divested her of her shirt.

"Can you make it home in five?" Thorn asked.

"Three," Cam vowed.

It was really more like two minutes before they stumbled into the bedroom where Cam and Thorn both proved they had absolutely no trouble sharing her or each other.

About the Author

৪০

The multi-published author of sizzling erotic romances, Shayla Black spends her "free" time as a reality TV junkie and reads everything she can get her eyes on. She also enjoys step aerobics and weightlifting, spending time with her family, and listening to an eclectic blend of music.

A writing risk-taker, Shayla is willing to try anything once and loves tackling a new writing challenge with every book. Emotion-based relationships and hot love scenes from the heart provide the foundation for all her books.

Shayla welcomes comments from readers. You can find her website and email address on her author bio page at www.ellorascave.com.

Tell Us What You Think

We appreciate hearing reader opinions about our books. You can email us at Comments@EllorasCave.com.

Why an electronic book?

We live in the Information Age—an exciting time in the history of human civilization, in which technology rules supreme and continues to progress in leaps and bounds every minute of every day. For a multitude of reasons, more and more avid literary fans are opting to purchase e-books instead of paper books. The question from those not yet initiated into the world of electronic reading is simply: *Why?*

1. *Price.* An electronic title at Ellora's Cave Publishing and Cerridwen Press runs anywhere from 40% to 75% less than the cover price of the exact same title in paperback format. Why? Basic mathematics and cost. It is less expensive to publish an e-book (no paper and printing, no warehousing and shipping) than it is to publish a paperback, so the savings are passed along to the consumer.

2. *Space.* Running out of room in your house for your books? That is one worry you will never have with electronic books. For a low one-time cost, you can purchase a handheld device specifically designed for e-reading. Many e-readers have large, convenient screens for viewing. Better yet, hundreds of titles can be stored within your new library—on a single microchip. There are a variety of e-readers from different manufacturers. You can also read e-books on your PC or laptop computer. (Please note that Ellora's Cave does not endorse any specific brands.

You can check our websites at www.ellorascave.com or www.cerridwenpress.com for information we make available to new consumers.)

3. *Mobility.* Because your new e-library consists of only a microchip within a small, easily transportable e-reader, your entire cache of books can be taken with you wherever you go.

4. *Personal Viewing Preferences.* Are the words you are currently reading too small? Too large? Too… ANNOYING? Paperback books cannot be modified according to personal preferences, but e-books can.

5. *Instant Gratification.* Is it the middle of the night and all the bookstores near you are closed? Are you tired of waiting days, sometimes weeks, for bookstores to ship the novels you bought? Ellora's Cave Publishing sells instantaneous downloads twenty-four hours a day, seven days a week, every day of the year. Our webstore is never closed. Our e-book delivery system is 100% automated, meaning your order is filled as soon as you pay for it.

Those are a few of the top reasons why electronic books are replacing paperbacks for many avid readers.

As always, Ellora's Cave and Cerridwen Press welcome your questions and comments. We invite you to email us at Comments@ellorascave.com or write to us directly at Ellora's Cave Publishing Inc., 1056 Home Avenue, Akron, OH 44310-3502.

Discover for yourself why readers can't get enough
of the multiple award-winning publisher

Ellora's Cave.

Whether you prefer e-books or paperbacks,

be sure to visit EC on the web at
www.ellorascave.com

for an erotic reading experience that will leave you
breathless.

2913820